BOSS

TUCKER MOORE

Copyright © 2023 by Tucker Moore.

All rights reserved. Except for brief quotations in a review, this book, or parts thereof, must not be reproduced in any form without permission in writing from the author. For information, address all queries to: atmoore75@gmail.com

First published 2023

ISBN: 979-8-218-24510-8

Printed in the United States of America

This was always for my brother, Jarrett

CONTENTS

One	1
Two	17
Three	32
Four	46
Five	60
Six	80
Seven	96
Eight	113
Nine	126
Ten	141
Eleven	152
Twelve	171
Thirteen	186

ONE

Cassandra stood with her back to the wall, between the water fountain and the large glass window that displayed the courtyard at the center of Seaside High. She glanced, somewhat bemused, into the small plaza, and rested her eyes on the centerpiece; an iron sculpture, a globe apparently, with an arrow pointing upward through it, where she had waited for Roman every school day since they began "officially" dating. Sometimes they saw each other before school in the parking lot, if their timing was right, but they had different lunch times and classes on different halls, so now, after first period, was the only time they could see each other at school.

Cassandra held an enormous biology textbook tightly across her chest as animated throngs of classmates jostled for precious space down the crowded locker-lined hall. People she knew passed her gesturing wildly, waving and grinning from their witty rejoinders. Relief was felt by all as they briskly moved on to the next class. She thought back over the few weeks she and Roman had been dating. He had changed, and it worried her. His mother had recently moved out. She wondered what that was like and thought of her own family.

Roman suddenly appeared around the corner, his book bag hanging to one side, and she looked at his shoulders and arms and watched him walk—she liked his walk—and they exchanged an amused glance. He came close to her and, kissing being forbidden at school, touched her arm. She remembered the first time she saw him, her first week at Seaside High, in the parking lot as he got out of his car and walked toward the school building. He looked like the usual intimidating senior who had important things to get to and a secret vast coterie of admirers. She had quickly walked on, but a little way off she had looked back over her shoulder and he was not watching her, though she had hoped he would be.

"Hello, there," he half said, half whispered.

"Hello, yourself."

"Class was boring," he groaned as they started to walk.

"It's Latin. It's supposed to be," she answered.

"I just don't know what it's supposed to be for," he said, faking exasperation.

Cassandra had no answer so she let the subject hang and then casually float away so she could ask what she wanted to. Roman, still puzzled, led them languidly and adjusted the bag on his shoulder. A locker slammed, they both started, and looked at the cause of the noise: another student, who glared at them. Looking back at each other, they laughed at themselves for being so jumpy.

"What was that?" Roman asked.

"I don't know," Cassandra said. "What are you doing after school?"

"Nothing much."

"What are you doing tonight?"

"No plans."

"My parents want me to go with them, but they said you could come over later."

Roman had first noticed Cassandra after school on the softball field. He was practicing with his own team when he looked over and a particular player caught his eye. He moved closer to get a better look, squinting in the late afternoon sun.

He had pondered an approach for a couple days. Aborting two planned accidental hallway encounters, he walked up to her a few days later and rather deliberately, after deciding he had to do something to ease his mind, clumsily asked her out. The words were garbled coming out of his mouth and for a second he wondered just what he had said. Nothing had sounded quite right or as he had rehearsed it.

"I'll have to ask my parents," she said.

Roman, confused at what he had just done but not regretting it, had not planned for that response so said quickly "okay," smiled, and walked away awkwardly. Cassandra, still puzzled, became embarrassed for him, realizing her friends had been standing right next to her and within earshot of the whole episode. She had smiled to herself, impressed by his courage.

The difference in their ages had concerned her parents. It was only after a lot of convincing on Cassandra's part that she had even been allowed to go on a date. Her mother was casual about it, but her father had been stern, wary in the way father are over their daughters, and his initial response was an emphatic "no." Finally, after much lobbying from Cassandra, who was determined that this was going to happen, Roman was allowed to come over for dinner. Cassandra had gotten her way. Her father greeted Roman severely at the door, but Roman was easily likeable, naturally polite, and he was charming and respectful in ways parents liked. He won them over. He returned every weekend until her parents finally let them go on a real "car" date. The couple went to a drive-up burger joint, determined the parking space "their space," and Cassandra was home by 9 p.m.

"What time should I be there?" Roman asked.

"Around seven."

They started walking toward the spot where they had to part. They only had minutes left.

"How's your day been?" she asked.

"Good. And yours?"

"Well, I was trying to listen to Mrs. Snow in English, but Teresa kept dropping notes on the floor in front of me, so I missed a whole section of the class on some Edgar Allan Poe poem about a bird."

Roman nodded.

"And, you know, I heard Holly say that some guy might be asking her to prom so I might know someone there my own age."

In a few short weeks Seaside High had scheduled the hallowed tradition that is The Prom. Roman had asked Cassandra to go with him. It was all she could think about; Roman, too. When she realized she had brought it up again she was slightly embarrassed, which Roman noticed, putting his arm around her. He knew she was excited about it. They both were. Cassandra had dreams of ivory adventures, scarlet silk dresses, sequins glittering in the moonlight.

Roman displayed a calm reserve, especially around his friends, but hated secretly when anyone said prom sucked. They had no romantic sense, he thought, but kept his own notions to himself. Roman had past proms to live with. He remembered going his sophomore year with a junior, Karen Peterson, a last-minute kind of thing, arranged by Taylor Jones. A girl he kind of had a crush on, which she knew, and, knowing this, knew he would do anything she asked and did so to help a friend of hers whose boyfriend had just broken up with her the week before prom. Roman barely knew Karen so, combined with an overall general awkwardness and an at-the-prom nervous out-of-place-ness, when beer was offered freely at a friend's house, he'd gotten piss drunk before being picked up and Karen had not seemed to mind.

When the opportunity arose, and the availability of some strong Everclear PJ made it easy, Karen retaliated by becoming inebriated in the same fashion and they made a miserable affair of it. The evening had started off quite well, Roman thought he remembered, before she started drinking. She had a flirty disposition toward him at first but things devolved quickly. Getting drunk was then a rather new experience. He—having only been drunk a handful of times, and not really knowing the consequences of having too much—had too much. It was his first time waking up somewhere and not knowing how he had gotten there.

Karen had passed out over the course of the night, after a brief excursion to the actual prom where they ignored each other. Most of the events were pieced together later over the following days.

"How's your dad?" Cassandra asked.

"I think he's getting better."

"That's good."

They walked a little further, to the point in the hall where they had to say goodbye.

"I just can't wait, is all," Cassandra admitted.

"Have I mentioned how much I love wearing a tuxedo?" he said with a humorous smile.

"Are you being sarcastic?"

"No. I genuinely like wearing a tuxedo," Roman said, but Cassandra gave him an unconvinced glance.

"We're going to have a great time," she said jubilantly.

Roman agreed with a nod. He took her hand and squeezed it tightly for a moment before he let it go. He watched as Cassandra appeared to dance away, disappearing around a sharp corner, looking back at him at the last moment over her shoulder.

Roman knew instantly, with a calmness of singular purpose, that he cared about her. He was stunned for a moment. Such thoughts were dangerous. Roman considered all this and somehow moved his mind away with a smile.

The edges were blurry, mostly not there at all. Something was coming into corporeal form, like binoculars focusing. A woman was there—no background, none was needed. She was exceptionally beautiful to him. The scene, though not fully realized, seemed to be behind glass streaked with rain drops, murky and translucent, but he was beginning to see. It was her.

It had been several months since she had visited the weary catacombs of Baron's sleep life, thanks to one milligram clonazapams in a drawer beside his bed. Baron had learned to revel in his nightly fantasies instead of rejecting them.

"It's good to see you," Baron whispered to the ghostly figure.

She made no reply and started to move away from him. Next time Baron would try to reach out, but not this time. He watched her with curiosity and an inert stillness uncommon for dreaming. Baron wondered if the memory of a person reoccurred solely for the benefit of the dreamer, or the memory itself. She looked back at him just before she vanished. Gone with her, too, was the feeling of joy. His happiness at one time had, after all, emanated mostly from her presence, hearing her breathing, listening to her voice, touching her hair.

Baron opened his eyes and heard the faint sound of a car driving by. Birds were chirping outside. He wondered offhand and randomly what kind they were. Through a small hole in the blinds the sun shone right on his face. He shifted a little in bed and looked over at the clock. It was earlier than he wished it was. He closed his eyes, hoping to fall back asleep and maybe dream about her again.

She was still his first waking thought every morning and once again he wondered if it would always be so. In sleep his mind was able to let her go, but the waking world was different. He still missed her. It had been a year since she had left. The ripping unexpectedness of her leaving had passed, but the whole question of why and what purpose it served, if there was any purpose to be served by it, lingered on as a foul, ever-present failure. He felt even worse for Roman and had since relied even more on his son as he himself had withdrawn from the world. As Baron had shown a prolonged grief, Roman had exuded strength. Baron closed his eyes more tightly, hoping to go back and get an answer he knew would never come.

Baron remembered that he had always gotten out of bed after her. He would roll over into the warm spot she had left. Once she asked him how he knew that he loved her. He responded with a smile and said, "How could I not?"

"That's a good answer," she said, giggling.

She came over to him, still in bed, and gave him a kiss.

"You think you're something with your good answers."

He sure was. It had been good to see her.

After a half hour he gave up on sleeping, got out of bed, and looked out the window. It had rained in the middle of the night. Baron scratched his head and yawned as he put on his bathrobe.

Baron was 47, tall and dark-haired. He was graying at the temples and his muscular build was clear due to the weight he had lost in the last year. He didn't look at all like the father of an eighteen-year-old. He had a week's worth of beard growing up from his neck to high on his cheeks. He went long periods without shaving. He passed the door to Roman's room; it was still closed. He went out behind the house to the garage.

Roman got up around eleven. It was a beautiful Saturday morning, and the warm sunlight was a prelude to the coming season. Roman spent the day at a friend's house lying around, watching TV and smoking cigarettes. Cassandra went last-minute shopping with her mother and, around 5:30, Roman picked her up, made nice with her family, uncomfortable during the taking of pictures, her little brother staring weirdly at him the whole time, and, as quickly as he could, got out of there.

He reluctantly brought Cassandra to his sad, empty house. Baron had insisted. Cassandra could be trusted to be delicate; she was good in that way. Baron liked her and was unusually talkative the few times he had seen her. Roman would leave them alone so they could talk, feeling an embarrassed awkwardness come over him when the three of them were together. The qualities of Roman's character that she was attracted to were apparent in Baron—a sensitivity and gentleness and a quiet shade of sorrow. She believed they had to have come from his father and had to be what Roman's mother had seen in him. Generations show a pattern.

"So, when are you going to be home?" Baron asked Roman.

"I don't know."

Baron looked at Cassandra.

"Just get this lovely young lady home early so her father doesn't have to worry about his little girl."

"I will," he said.

A garish white stretch limo pulled up in front of the small yellow house and the horn blew. They said their goodbyes and walked outside.

"Roman, we should take him with us," she whispered.

"He'll be fine," he said, giving his father a slight wave goodbye.

The back window rolled slowly down with a soft electric whine, smoke wafting out first, then music and excitable voices escaped, and Miles stuck his head out.

"Your chariot has arrived," he said, a devilish smirk on his face and a lit cigarette, its end glowing orange, hanging from the corner of his mouth. Roman and Cassandra hurried down the driveway, time being so precious, and Baron stood on the porch, a rare ease in his eyes, as they drove away. The limo sped along the streets, out of the sleeping suburbs, into the spring night of the city.

The limo pulled into the parking lot of the Seaside Moose Lodge building just after nine. Roman got out first, followed by Cassandra. Miles and his date, Betty, were followed by Drew and his date, Patricia. They had just come from dinner at an expensive but rather generic restaurant at which the sextet had dined on their parents' dime and barely ate anything at all. Miles and Drew had taken turns going to the bathroom to take pulls from a bourbon-filled flask. Halfway through dinner, Betty and Patricia gave in and decided to join them. Roman and Cassandra had declined and spent most of dinner watching their excited companions. Cassandra, a freshman, didn't know Betty and Patricia that well. Betty and Patricia were always together, had even decided on dating Miles and Drew together. Miles and Drew, also best friends, were similarly always together.

Miles and Drew had been run out of the bar area after attempting to purchase drinks. The bartender was obviously aware that it was prom night and the two gentlemen were underage.

"You can't blame us for trying," Drew kept saying, as Patricia scolded him for embarrassing her. After a private tongue-lashing from their girlfriends in private corners of the restaurant, Drew, Patricia, Miles, and Betty returned to the table. Drew and Miles at first looked dour but as they caught a glimpse of one another they burst out laughing. Roman suggested they get the check. After the warning, Drew and Miles started to cling to their dates on the way out, saying they were sorry. Once in the car all was forgiven and Patricia and Betty resumed taking grimacing swigs from the flasks.

"Come on, Roman! Take one, you sissy, you Nancy boy."

Roman shook his head.

"Go ahead, I don't care," Cassandra said.

Roman took the flask and took a swig. He almost spewed it back out immediately, but he managed to hold it down. Miles, Drew, Betty, and Patricia all laughed heartily as Roman coughed. He had to take it, so he laughed with them. One would be enough to get this red-faced, devilish duo off his back for a while.

Once they were all out of the limo, Roman, head swirling a bit, looked up, and saw the Hale–Bopp comet was still up there in the sky. From it he looked down at his date. Cassandra's thick dark hair was up in a tight ball behind her head. She was beautiful. Her tea-length solid white, satin dress with a slightly trailing hemline was cut tightly and perfectly fit her slender frame. It was strapless and cut straight across her chest, showing her neck, collarbones, and smooth, tanned shoulders. He took her hand, and they followed the other couples in.

The old Moose Lodge building was a stale, blocky brick box built for an older, blander, generation of veterans. It was not nearly as ritzy as the Ramada from last year, Roman thought. Scotch taped decorations and draped fabric were the best the prom committee could do. It was like any other prom. Tables spread out, a punch bowl here, a DJ there. Music, a dance floor, and dark were really all that was needed. There were the juniors, most at their first prom, nervous and confused. The seniors, cutting loose a bit, having been there and done that, at their final prom. Prom was many things; a shedding of one's school identity, a costume party of pretense, a social hurdle, a phony genteel proving ground, Roman thought, an evening eternally regretted.

"What in the hell happened?" Miles asked offhand as they got to the door.

"I heard we didn't plan well enough," Patricia said.

"We?" Miles said. "I didn't know anything about it."

"Like you would have done something about it," Betty said, shoving him.

"I might have," Miles responded while holding the door open and they all laughed as they went in.

They presented their prom tickets to the teacher at the door. "Who did you go to the prom with?" Roman heard one of the chaperones ask another teacher as he walked by. I'm still married to her. The group said hello to the teachers at the main entrance and foyer and then went into the main room. It was dimly lit, with a refreshment table at one end and a stage at the other. There were round tables on both sides of the room, which left an area in front of the stage for a dance floor. Roman saw that there were already a number of people there—half of whom he had never seen before. It was a very large high school. They moved through the room and passed people standing about, lolling here and there. Their gazes were indecipherable and vacant. They were all strangers really, and the major part of their lives was away from school and known only to those who lived them. They shared—only briefly—a common hallway at an educational factory.

Roman said hello and nodded to some guys he recognized from the junior class. He then moved on to another group of his friends, Cassandra following close behind.

Even as dark as it was, the room was still oppressive—cold and utilitarian. The cinderblock walls were painted nicotine yellow and the floor was a grimy tile that had once been white. The place felt neglected, the paintings and framed pictures on the walls had old names on them and the photos were in black and white.

The dancing began solemnly. "This place is a nightmare," Roman heard someone comment.

"It's prom hell," another said, which made Roman and Cassandra look at one another and laugh. It was true, but the building itself would soon be as forgotten as the finer details of the night would be years hence.

"Jennifer is here," Cassandra pointed out.

"Who?" Roman asked.

"A girl I know."

"Go talk to her."

Roman looked around for someone he could talk to. He saw Stuart from the golf team, so he shifted a little to the left and stood beside him. The thump of dance music began, and the dance floor filled.

"I thought you were going to sit this one out," Roman said.

"She made me come," he responded, pointing his head in some vague direction.

Roman smiled, knowing he would hear that one often tonight.

"Don't you look fancy," Stuart said, giving him his full attention. Stuart was wearing a suit, which made Roman feel awkward.

"It's the tux," Roman said, gripping it by the lapels. "Come on, Stuart, say it. It's fun."

"Say what?"

"Cummberbund."

"It's pronounced 'cummerbund,' " Stuart said.

Cassandra came back and Roman nodded to Stuart as he walked away.

"Some people aren't in a very good mood," Roman said.

"Like who?" she asked.

"Just people in general," Roman answered, feeling angry about being corrected.

Roman met up again with Miles, Drew, Betty, and Patricia, sweating and out of breath from the dance floor. A wild giddiness enveloped them, and they galloped away.

"What time do we take pictures?" Roman heard someone ask.

"Ten."

"Good. I can't wait to get out of here," Miles said, "I'm going to the bathroom."

"Wait," Drew said after thinking about it. "I'm coming, too."

Roman and Cassandra stood around for a while as the number of tuxedos and gowns swelled around the edges of the dance floor. Miles and Drew came back. They were now dancing as they walked, bobbing around like two idiots. Suddenly the music changed to a slow song and the dance floor emptied.

"I want to dance," Cassandra yelled over the music and pulled at his arm.

"We can't be the only ones out there," Roman tried to say.

"Everyone wants to dance, they just need someone to do it first," she said, dragging him out to the middle of the floor.

"Poor bastard," Miles mumbled as he watched Roman and Cassandra walk toward the dance floor.

"Why do you say that?" Betty asked.

"Roman. He makes me laugh. He tries to be so perfect."

"At least he's trying."

"Harrumph. He's just trying to get in her pants."

"He is not," she retorted, slapping his arm.

"We all are."

"You're not getting in these."

"We'll see about that."

"They look cute together."

"It'll never last."

"Don't be so negative."

"Trust me. I know Roman better than you do."

Roman and Cassandra put their arms around the other and danced. Other couples joined in as a group formed around them. Roman and Cassandra were close but said nothing, listening to the music. The song over, the DJ upped the tempo and, not ready for all-out dancing, they laughed, shook their heads, and Roman pulled her by the hand off the floor. They relaxed among a group just on the edge of the dance floor. They walked, still holding hands, and encountered acquaintances of Roman's. Cassandra was introduced and smiled that wide smile of hers and all were charmed. Roman was having a great time. He started to wish that last year's prom hadn't been such a disaster.

There was Simon—the valedictorian he had sat beside in band during his middle school years—who couldn't locate his date. And there were others, all bringing back memories of when he had done this or that, and he thought about who he had been then and who he was now. In the bathroom he had run into Drew and had taken a couple swigs of whiskey in a stall.

He came out and saw Cassandra, waiting and looking breathless, so they went to a table to sit down and take a break when Roman suddenly saw someone who, in all the newness and confusion, had completely, and finally, slipped his mind. Sandy Wellman. His ex-girlfriend whom he had dated from about mid-sophomore year to the end of junior year, just before his mother had left. Sandy was stunning in her long red gown and a quake went through his heart. The guy she was with went to another high school and they had been together since she and Roman had broken up. Roman tried to look away as he saw her look in his direction. He could feel her momentary gaze. When he glanced over at her, as if she could sense his gaze, she quickly looked away. Roman wondered how many other people were getting funny looks from people. After he and Sandy broke up Roman had not gone on more than a few dates with any one girl until Cassandra came along and broke him out of his slump.

"Who was that?" Cassandra asked suddenly.

"Nobody," he said.

Roman looked around and realized the prom is the one night a person practically goes on a date with every girl he has ever dated. It was interesting to see the guy who had replaced him. He saw the first girl he ever kissed, in middle school, Erin Meadows, who back then had told everyone he did not know how to kiss properly. In the everyday it's easy to avoid an ex by just steering clear of them and being around different people.

He thought again of Sandy Wellman. When they dated early on, she wouldn't have sex with him. At the time she wanted to be married first. Roman had nodded agreement, himself a little scared of the notion, and went along with it and respected her for it but eventually he became selfish and curious. At the time everyone around Roman was talking sex and about what people had done sex-wise; rumors were flying around school about everybody. The grand irony of the thing was after he and Sandy broke up, she supposedly had done it with this new boyfriend soon afterwards. He shuddered. It is odd, he thought. He would have to avoid her all night. He had been doing it for the last two years.

They took pictures at ten. The hour after that was a black and white blur to Roman. Everything happened so fast. One face, another face, and then a "this is so-and-so." He couldn't count the number of people he met or the conversations he listened to.

"Did you see the dress on so-and-so?"

"It's horrible."

"She's here by herself."

"No way!"

"Did you see the girl with her brother?"

"Where is a good place to smoke this joint?"

"Man, I'm high as hell already."

"I had no idea she was so hot."

"I tried to tell you, dude."

"She's bustin' out of that dress."

"I can't believe her dad let her leave the house in that thing."

Roman was staring off into the crowd on the dance floor when Cassandra came up to him.

"Come on."

"What time is it?"

"Midnight."

The three couples piled back into the limo and were soon being whisked to their next destination, Miles's house, in the upscale Seaside neighborhood of Rexwood. His divorced father was conveniently out of town visiting his girlfriend in the big city, as Miles told it. In the limo, the three couples held each other closely and were in their own little worlds, whispering about this and that. Miles and Betty started to make out. Drew and Patricia did the same, not to be one-upped. Roman and Cassandra just giggled nervously at one another. Roman was happy that he and his two best friends and their girls had experienced a normal prom. No panic, drama, or disappointment.

Getting out of the limo they stumbled up to the house through the dark until Miles found his key. He opened the door, and they went into silence, the hum of the prom music still in their ears.

"Mi casa es su casa," he instructed as they opened a bottle of wine in a well-lit kitchen. A glass was poured for everyone. Roman held his. Cassandra took a sip and without a word or look they all scattered to the utmost privacy of the enormous house of the lawyer dad and forgot about each other.

Roman and Cassandra crept up the stairs to the master bedroom, as Roman and Miles had arranged beforehand. Roman took off his coat, turned on the TV, and kicked off his shoes as Cassandra did the same. They both crawled onto the bed.

"I had a great time tonight, I mean, awesome," Roman said.

"You were so handsome and were such a gentleman," Cassandra said musically.

"It was the tux."

"You think you'll go with me to the prom next year?" she asked. Roman hadn't thought of that. He didn't see why not.

"Of course I will," he answered.

"Even if you're off at school somewhere?"

"I told you, Cassandra, I'm not going anywhere. I'm going to stay right here in Seaside, go to the community college until you graduate, then we'll go somewhere together."

"You promise?"

"You promise me you won't think I'm some dope for waiting around for you," he said.

"I would never think that. You're the best thing that's ever happened to me."

Roman thought for a minute, remembering the desperate feeling he had had earlier.

"What if I said I love you?" Roman asked.

"I love you, too," was her reply.

It was their first time saying it to each other.

"I want to," she whispered in his ear.

"Let's wait," he said. We have all the time in the world, let's not rush things," he said. It was what he had rehearsed. It was simple. She would be happy and he would be happy. He hoped so, anyway.

For a moment he felt a terrible feeling that she would feel rejected, but when she smiled and he sensed that she was relieved, he felt better about it. He knew she was willing to be with him. He wanted her to trust him more and then decide for herself. She was so young and Roman knew, in the short years of the future, what it would mean for both of them. And the room was silent, the air was hushed and cool, and sounds of people moving about the house could be heard, life and love were present, and ghosts of proms past were swept away in the glow of the streetlight through the window.

TWO

It was the first warm Saturday of April and for Augustus that meant the beginning of a new era in his life. The sun had fallen to just above the distant pine trees and hung there, perfect and red. Along the road he passed fenced pastures; grazing horses; loitering cows; scattered white farmhouses; fading, half-collapsed tobacco barns. The fields had recently been plowed under and the crops would soon be planted. As his thoughts swirled the land went unnoticed, but not the time. Augustus drove fast down Highway 34, the top of his Chevy Corvette down, the radio blasting and wind in his hair. His baseball uniform fluttered around in the seat beside him; he grabbed it just before it blew away and threw his baseball glove on top of it. The air turned cool as he moved into a shadowed tunnel of dark pines. Augustus shuddered, signaled left, and passed a white minivan doing the speed limit. As he swung around the van he looked at the driver, who returned a reproachful glance. He responded by stomping on the accelerator and shot away. The feeling of reproach faded and dread crept once again over him as he looked up and saw a magnificent sky. The sun peeked through a cumulus cloud and the light fell to places unseen. Predictable and sustaining was the world's constancy and he looked to it often for comfort. He imagined his own absence from it and felt a vague terror.

    He thought about the team and tonight's game and pressed the accelerator a little more. His eyes felt heavy, his insomnia had gotten worse. He wondered if he should tell someone. Would anyone hear him when everything looked, on the outside, so normal? He wished people would stop reminding him how awesome it was to be young in that jovial, sarcastic way people do. His reverie passed as the sun returned and Augustus looked up into in his rearview mirror at himself for a recklessly long time and watched a grin mature into something mocking.

This new era would be different, he thought. He would commit himself to a new beginning, a new life. He sought perpetually, desperately, to move his thoughts forward, but he was destined, it seemed to always be fixed in the past, frozen in a recurring, bewildered instant. He felt he had navigated the freefall of the last three years of high school as well as anyone. No one would believe how hard he was trying.

He pushed a cassette tape Nora had made into the stereo and their well-worn song played. It reminded him that he had failed to be the person he wanted to be. Nora was that weird mystery of discovered possibilities. He had been at Nora's house all afternoon. She had brought an element of knowledge to his life, but also chaos. Augustus had fallen in love immediately. But, sadly, that had not always been enough. He had kissed her goodbye, but her smile was labored as he left. She was still guarded at times and he could sense it. It was his own fault; he knew it in ways he could not admit consciously. Still, he was reassured because the afternoon had been composed and leisurely. This time would be his last chance to make things what they should have always been. Everything he wanted depended on it and he was hopeful. Nora would be at the game tonight, sitting with her friends in the bleachers, the night cool and soft, filled with the sudden echoing cheers.

The car careened down the road, the smooth air rushing past him. Behind him leaves on the road swirled and spun. He had advantages that felt undeserved, unearned. From birth, of course, he'd had no real choice. He was who he was. He was Hart's son. He pressed down on the accelerator further and the speedometer hit 75.

Leaving Nora's he passed the place where the daffodils had bloomed. He remembered her pointing them out when they had first started dating. He had never noticed them. Since then, he had looked for them. They were withered now but he had seen them bloom this year. The tiny yellow flowers had flickered by, beneath a canopy of tall pines. When they did bloom cars could be seen parked alongside the road with people milling about. There was a sign nailed to a tree with the words "Do Not Pick" painted in black letters. He had picked them anyway.

Augustus had a baseball game to get to. Baseball seemed a remote, silly thing; he could feel his love for it dying. He saw that love still in others and found it amusing—somewhat pathetic. He was already regretting his decision to sign a letter of intent to play baseball at NC State. Numbness filled him when he thought too much about it. Even back during football season. At his final football game some seniors had cried when they won the state championship. He had only shrugged it off and gone home.

Before baseball season even started, he had thought seriously about not playing. His father would never have let that happen because of the potential for a scholarship, which made no sense since his father was the wealthiest man in town. What he really wanted to do was be in Europe with his friends, who were there now on the Spring Break school trip. Europe would have to wait; he and Nora had plans to go together. The speedometer hit 90 and the rushing wind roared.

He had played because he could see how hurt his teammates might be. He couldn't tolerate their disapproval or the tumult it would lead to. He had gone to the college signing ceremony, with cameras and the media present, and automatically, as if controlled remotely, wore his Liberty High T-shirt, smiled and shook hands, and made everyone happy. He had committed to playing baseball in college, yet his mind still wandered. At least he knew where he was going for the next four years. He'd thought it would make Nora happy, because they'd be going to the same college, but that day her reaction was subdued.

Houses were blinking past him, and he slowed down as the darkening forest surrounded him. He came out of it and into a clearing on both sides, where he saw the Coxville city limits sign. The road started to slope downward and to the left—Augustus slowed. There was only one stoplight in Coxville. The town's most prominent feature was a large red brick church on a hill on one of the main intersection's corners. The church loomed, as if it were watching over the town. Across the intersection on the opposite corner was the glimmering glass of the car dealership building and the bright, crisp new cars. In the weary dusk it all looked lonely and beyond reproach.

Augustus was stopped at the intersection by the red light. On the other two corners of the intersection stood an old, abandoned service station and the two-story crumbling red brick A. G. Forlines building that housed the local hardware store. Augustus wondered why they didn't just tear those old buildings down. The car dealership was his father Hart's, and before him it had belonged to Hart's father, Augustus Senior. Augustus could see that the gates were still open. He looked over and saw his father's truck parked up near the building in its usual spot. Monday through Saturday they were open until seven and it was just about six. Hart was probably still at his desk. There were two chairs across from the desk and one was always occupied by his grandfather, Augustus Senior. Augustus, too, had been spending more and more time opposite his father and the desk. He did not see his grandfather's truck.

Hart was the mayor of Coxville, a little boomtown swelling every day with new houses and families. Its larger neighbor to the west, Martinsboro, had a growing university with medical and engineering schools. Augustus Senior owned vast tracts of land around the town where new roads were laid, and skeletal wooden frames rose like tombstones. Fresh new paint dried, green sod was laid, swing sets were set up, and new cars arrived in bright, clean, concrete driveways. The cheerful new homes rose, treeless, where tobacco had once dominated the landscape of Augustus Senior's generation. Augustus made a left turn and headed out of town toward the high school.

Nora watched from her porch as Augustus backed out of her driveway. As he went by, he stuck his hand out the window and waved. She waved back. She was glad he had gone slowly and knew what he was thinking as he sped away. Years ago, the neighbors had complained about her lead-footed boyfriend speeding furiously down the residential streets. Nora pulled her sweater tighter.

She was a beautiful girl. Her long, curly blonde hair was matched with large blue eyes. She was smart, too, class valedictorian. The boys in her class all had crushes. She was capricious and whimsical with them, and they loved her more for it. She was friendly to all and a bit flirtatious in way that sometimes, with less open-minded persons, earned her rebuke. She was wickedly perceptive and would say shocking things out loud. She was misunderstood by all and difficult to read. Her accent was harsh, quick and direct. She was well-liked, envied even, but many could be intimidated by her otherness. She was the only girl in the entire class from "up north," a fact that she was very proud of in a sometimes insufferable, privileged way. She'd ended up at Liberty High, a rural school outside of Coxville, by pure chance. As it was, she made most of her friends from the more affluent girls who went to the city school, Scott High, in Martinsboro.

She climbed the porch steps, saw the swing and, even though she was a little cold, decided that since she hadn't sat in it for a while, she would. She leaned against the chain on one side and brought her legs up on the seat. She sat sideways in the swing and rested her head on the chain, wrapped with tie-dyed cloth, and looked out at the still homes and yards. From her house the daily lives of some four or five neighbors could be watched. She saw Mr. Rhodes across the street getting out of his car, carrying his briefcase and a bag of groceries. She wondered how he was getting along; she had recently found out that his wife had died, of what she didn't know, and he was now raising an infant daughter alone. Next door to him was the Simmons family. She had known their oldest son, who was two years ahead of her in school. She tried to remember his name. Ben. It was Ben. She tried to imagine what he could be doing now, what his life after high school was like. She had many friends who had gone off to college and she talked to them occasionally, but they seemed far off and not themselves anymore. They had changed, she supposed.

She heard barking from the yard behind her house, masked by evergreens. She knew nothing of the homeowners; their cars appeared at night and disappeared early in the morning. The dog was a small one she had never seen. She got up and went to the door to let her own dog out. Napoleon had been hers since she could remember, and he was now growing old. When she went back to sit in the swing Napoleon curled up on her bare feet as if he knew they were getting cold. Napoleon's head rose up and Nora saw that a boy on a bicycle was coming. She watched him pedal by, she herself hidden from the road by the shrubs surrounding her house. She wondered if it was wrong to spy on people in such a way.

Nora had moved from Connecticut the summer after her eighth-grade year, when her father found a job outside of Martinsboro. Being uprooted was a blow from which Nora felt she was still rebounding. The cold feeling of being a stranger, every day, made her look on everything with detachment. She felt the true transience of her small life. Slowly, after recovering from an uncharacteristic decline, she was able to be happy again in North Carolina. She had always made friends fast.

Nora heard a car door slam shut and she and Napoleon turned to see that it was her mother, who had just pulled into the driveway.

Napoleon jumped up and moved to greet her, barking and wagging his tail.

"Hey there," her mother said to him and then looked up and saw Nora in the swing.

"I see you," she said, smiling up at her.

Nora beamed. "You need some help?"

"No, I'm fine."

"Been out shopping?"

"Oh, I picked up a few things," she said, climbing the porch steps, bags in her hands.

"You want to sit?" Nora asked.

"Sure. What are you doing out here?" she asked after Nora had moved to make room for her as she placed a kiss on her daughter's head.

"It's such a nice day."

"You should put a coat on. It's going to get cooler."

"Didn't want to get up. I was just getting cozy."

"What's going on?" her mother asked, rubbing Nora's shoulder.

"Nothing, really. Just spying on the neighbors."

"Has Augustus been here?" her mother asked, knowing the answer.

"How can you tell?"

"I can always tell."

"You think you're so smart," Nora quipped.

"I have my moments," her mother said after a while. "And how is your Southern beau?"

"Okay. Things are good now," Nora tried to say convincingly.

"Just be careful, is all."

"I will, and thanks for letting him come over last night."

"Just don't forget the way things have been. I can't take seeing you hurt anymore."

"So much for forgive and forget."

"I wish you could sweetie, I really wish you could."

"It's going to be different this time. He seems really different. He's grown up a lot."

Her mother shook her head.

"That is one boy I don't think I will ever understand. Smart, good looking. His family seems normal enough."

"His dad puts a lot of pressure on him."

"I'm sorry, honey, I'm just afraid he will, just out of the blue, change, like in the past. I'm not saying it's impossible, it's just you both have to be so careful around each other. You have so much history."

Nora listened, not really knowing what was right. That's what she and Augustus had agreed on. You just have to be hopeful, she thought.

"I'm going in. Want to come?" her mother asked.

"No. I want to sit here a little while longer."

"Okay," her mother said as she got up and carried her bags inside.

As Nora watched her go in, she thought of her mother's voice and how her own was nothing like it. Her mother always spoke in a calm, half asleep manner as if she had just risen for the day. It was a far-off and delicate voice. Augustus believed she was the most at ease person ever born, and that had always made him nervous. She was very different in every way from his own mother. He had discovered something suspicious about his parents—that they were often less than kind. Nora's mother was witty and playful; his own was severe and direct, businesslike. Nora's mother's laugh was faint and was always just at hand. She had a keen sense of humor and was an ironic jester—something she had passed on to her daughter. If you could make her laugh, you knew you had said something clever—and often even when you didn't know you had. She and Nora sparred often. There, in the finality of the day, Nora felt the cool solitude of her rootless existence and shivered, and wondered just who she really was.

Crack.

"Augustus, heads up, it's coming to you!" the coach shouted from the dugout.

Augustus brought his attention back to the game. He looked up, searching the sky desperately. He saw nothing. In the luminescence of the field's lights, he finally saw the little white speck of ball hovering above him. He had been stargazing instead of paying attention. It was a moonless night. The players had long sleeves on under their jerseys and the bleachers were filled with people in hats, sweaters, and coats.

His eyes searched the celestial void. Beyond the towers of glaring lights, he looked to the wisp of comet that hung like an errant splash of white paint in the night. He had tried to focus on the game, but he just kept turning to look at it. Augustus knew its sojourn through the summer nights would soon end. And every night it moved lower. He would miss it when it was gone. He remembered when it had first appeared a few months ago; he and Nora snuck out after their parents were asleep and went to an old graveyard in the middle of a field. They drank wine pilfered from Nora's parents and talked until Comet Hale-Bopp finally came up over the horizon.

"Neat, isn't it?" she had said.

"It makes you think," Augustus replied.

Sometimes, within Augustus, when he was with Nora, was the feeling that he was at a desk in a classroom, and she was the teacher. With her a whole new world of experiences had been opened to him. In the graveyard she pointed out constellations: the Big Dipper; Cassiopeia, the upside-down queen; and Polaris, the North Star. She liked horoscopes and tarot cards, New Age meditations on personal energy, and yoga. Her interests were infinite and kaleidoscopic. Her fantasies spilled out uninterrupted, and Augustus wanted to explore all of her fantastic whims with her.

Back in the game, Augustus put his glove up and the ball hit it with a thud. Cheers echoed off the tall pines. Augustus looked there into the dark trees standing in somber obedience, just beyond the edge of the lights. He shivered as he threw the ball to the infield and jogged to the dugout.

A large crowd was gathered. The public schools took their spring break around the time of the Crucifixion. For as long as anyone could remember, Scott High held an Easter baseball tournament on its home field during that week. Liberty High, two other high schools in the county, and two teams from nearby counties were invited. Scott High was the largest school both in funding and student body, not to mention first in the hearts and minds of those who went there and, secretly, of those who didn't. Scott High had won the tournament every year; they had a prestigious program, known throughout the state, with at least three or four players who had gone on to play at the collegiate level and a few drafted into the Major Leagues. Just being on the team at Scott could make a player better. Their field was magnificent, and the grandstands were the largest in eastern North Carolina. Tonight, the stands were overflowing, with spectators spilling out along the fences. Pro scouts as well. The smell of paper cups, hot dogs, and popcorn filled the air. Tonight was the championship game.

For years Augustus had gone with Hart to the tournament and the championship game. Hart himself had never played baseball but he loved the sport, and he remembered its absence from his own high school days. Augustus Senior had never cared for sports; he was always working. Instead of joining the teams Hart had spent every afternoon working for Augustus Senior. Work had always been the family's center; they needed everyone, sunup to sundown. Augustus Senior had lived through the Depression and World War II, in the navy, and felt money was the most important thing. Hart wanted something different for his son. Augustus remembered one game in particular when he was in eighth grade. He was at the game with a friend when

Liberty High's clean-up hitter, the gigantic Cal Thompson, had come to bat and crushed a home run over the light posts. The ball was never seen coming down; it had simply disappeared over the trees and into the darkness. That home run had been talked about ever since.

In the bottom of the seventh inning, it was Augustus's turn to bat. The score was zero to zero. When he walked up to the plate, he passed his teammate Aaron, who had struck out. Augustus had never really taken the game all that seriously, which had led to friction between him and his coaches. It was supposed to be fun, he thought, but it was more than that—to hear the crowd's adulation, the frenzy of cheers, the claps of approval.

He looked up at the scoreboard, could hear the lights' electric hum, and noticed a blown bulb in the home team's zero. He looked at the third base coach and the first base coach. The head coach at first gave him the signal to swing away, as Augustus had known he would. He took two practice swings and stepped into the batter's box. There were two outs. He kept his eyes on Jimmy Grimes, Scott's star pitcher, headed to the same college team as Augustus, to see if he would look at him. No, Jimmy was focused. Augustus didn't know Jimmy that well, they moved it different circles, but they knew of each other, and Augustus knew Jimmy wanted to strike him out. They both were tall and strong, good runners with excellent hand-eye coordination. Augustus had already struck out three times.

The pitch came. Ball one.

Augustus stepped out of the box, relieved. Jimmy had pinpoint accuracy; he was a lefty with a wicked curve ball. Augustus started to do his routine again, but he stopped and could feel something change. He was curious. He wanted to know if Nora was watching. He knew where she was sitting so, he turned slightly and looked for her; she was sitting in the third row up beside her friend Emily. The girls on either side of her were talking to her simultaneously. Nora was looking at him.

He could hear the coach clapping loudly, calling his name. "Augustus! Let's go!" The coach gave him the signal to swing away again. He tried to relax and stepped into the box. The second pitch came and Augustus watched it whiz by. Ball two.

He stepped out of the box and glanced down the first baseline fence for his father and grandfather. They were there as usual, side by side, with the other fathers of the Liberty players. Elbows on the fence and caps on their heads, watching intently.

He stepped back in the box. The third pitch came. Ball three.

Augustus saw that Jimmy was frustrated. Augustus now knew the coach had told Jimmy to just walk him. Imagine being the best pitcher in the state and being forced to walk someone.

Augustus stepped back in the box and waited patiently; he knew that Jimmy wanted to throw at least one strike. Augustus looked over at the third base coach. He got the sign to take the pitch and walk to first base. Augustus's teammates on the bench watched with frozen, worried faces. Their eyes moved from Augustus to Coach Winston.

"Do you think he'll swing?" someone whispered. "He better not," the assistant coach said to the players in the dugout.

Augustus got back into the box and took a practice swing. A sly grin that no one could have seen went across his face. Jimmy rocked back, cradled the ball to his chest, his leg kicked high, all in a smooth form of moving, his wind up mechanically perfect, swanlike, the arm extended, and came forward with a hard grace. The ball left his fingers, the rotation backward, with everything Jimmy had left, and hurtled at Augustus like a bullet. Augustus could see the little red stitches spinning, knowing it was a fastball. Jimmy was trying to throw one by him. Augustus stepped forward and swung. His fists and muscles tightened, and his head and eyes were steady as his arms came around. The bat itself was a silver blur when he heard the contact; he knew.

Augustus started to walk toward first base. He could barely track the ball with his eyes, but he got a sense of it. He could hear his coach yelling at him to run, but he just watched as the small white sphere streaked up and up into the night, reaching its apogee, then softly starting its descent into the pines beyond the left field fence. Augustus began to jog around the bases while the Scott High players kicked at the dirt, hands on hips in disbelief, fists punching gloves, or stood there, with nothing at all to do. He passed the first baseman, who turned his back and wouldn't look at him, and then the second baseman, who glared at him. Augustus looked at the ground. Often a gracious player would be congratulatory, but not anyone from Scott. It was supposed to be their night, their fifth straight championship. Sorry guys, Augustus thought, game over.

As Augustus touched second, he thought he heard thunder in the distance. He took another look into the stands and saw Nora. He tried to grasp the weight of the past, to see if he was happy enough to deal with it. He wasn't.

Hart and Augustus Senior watched the ball fly out of the park. Both were leaning forward, their arms resting on the top of the first baseline fence, where they stood for every game. Neither Augustus Senior or Hart had ever played the game, and both sometimes felt, at the same time, without knowing it or speaking of it, an irrevocable sense of loss when they watched Augustus play. When Hart was growing up and the other boys his age were playing baseball, he had been working at the farm or pumping gas at his father's station. He remembered days past—high school homecomings and pep rallies—with an alienation that seemed to come out of the ether. In high school he remembered watching, gas nozzle in hand, as the small homecoming parade came down Main Street, seeing the players and cheerleaders pass and wave at him from the street. Hart had been determined that Augustus would have all those things he had not. He had spent long hours with Augustus in the yard tossing a football in the fall and throwing a baseball come spring. He was proud of his son's success.

Augustus touched home plate and received the congratulations of his teammates. The frenzy and euphoria soon abated, and people shifted to gather their things, say a few last words, gather the children playing beneath the bleachers, and begin the walk to the parking lot. The buzz from the field lights hummed in the background.

After the game Augustus and Nora walked to the parking lot, the sound of gravel beneath their feet. Hart followed with Sarah, Augustus's mother. Their conversation, mattering in a way known only to them, was the warm noise of life. Augustus was far off and absorbed beyond reach in melancholy about what was and what was not, and could never be recovered.

"Let's go out tonight," he said.

"And do what?" Nora asked.

"The guys have some beer. Let's go hang with them."

"You know I don't like to drink," she said.

"You don't have too," Augustus responded.

"I don't want to sit around and watch you drink, either."

"I thought we talked about doing more things together," he retorted.

"What I meant was the little things we do together, not the getting stupid drunk kind of things."

Augustus couldn't stop thinking about the things he had heard about her drinking when they were broken up. He had heard all about those wild times. It was the side of her he had never really seen, had been too scared to let himself see.

"Please. I don't want fight, Augustus," she said, putting her arm around him and leaning against him.

"I don't know," he said "I just thought we might do something different?"

"I'm tired," she said, taking his arm and resting her head on his shoulder as they walked. "And besides, you just won the championship… beating Scott… hitting the game-winning home run. Jeez…isn't that enough for one night?"

The question lingered in Augustus's mind as they got into his Corvette and drove in silence through the glimmering, half-hidden shadow of night to Nora's house. They tiptoed as quietly as they could up the carpeted first flight of stairs, then the wooden steps of the second flight to her attic room. They listened for a moment to see if Nora's parents would wake but heard nothing—all was clear. Nora turned on the small TV on the dresser and they laid down on the futon in front of it. In the white noise Nora soon fell asleep and Augustus gently eased himself away, careful not to wake her. It was sixteen minutes after midnight. He put a blanket on her, kissed her head, and silently went out of her room and down the steps. He walked through her house as quietly as possible, opened the door, and went out onto the porch and looked to the streetlight on the corner. The Pines was dark, still, and sleepy, but he wasn't. He turned the key and his Corvette rumbled. He looked one last time up at Nora's window and backed out of the driveway. He came to the stop sign at the exit of The Pines and looked both ways. Going left meant home, playing it safe, doing the right thing, and tossing and turning in bed. Augustus turned right, thinking there had to be some beer left in that keg.

THREE

On a fresh May Saturday Nora awoke into a green morning beneath a pale blue sky, to the sounds of warmth and spring. Her mother and father had gone out early that morning to the boat her father was restoring at a marina thirty minutes away. After having breakfast at the table out on the back porch beneath the first cool rays of sun, Nora came back in the house and opened all the first-floor windows. There was a breeze blowing through the house, making the curtains ripple. Outside there was a pulse of grasshoppers, the whistle of a bird, and shimmering trees, their branches billowing with each light gust. Opening all the windows was something Nora had seen her mother do, she called it spring cleaning—with a wink—because she never did any cleaning. "Your father makes enough for me to be liberated from it," she would say. Nora's mother kept herself busy reading, painting, doing the yard work, and had a part-time job at an art gallery. She spent many hours tending her vegetable and flower gardens, her fruit trees, and grapevines, in the summer. She also kept a small greenhouse, nestled behind the house, its walls silvery with opaque plastic, smelling of soil and green fibers, which she would disappear into for long hours when it turned cool in the fall and throughout the winter.

Nora lived in a two-story side gabled white Victorian-style house with a deep wood-planked porch that ran around the entire first floor. The house was on the corner of Crestline and Maraschino, with a wide lawn, uncommon for the neighborhood, and an adjacent two-car garage that smelled of sawdust, where her father spent his time, when not in his upstairs office. The house was uncorrupted by its slightly out-of-place granite and shore-themed landscaping—a sensibility and atmosphere brought from Connecticut to the haphazard lanes of Mossy Oaks, part of the booming suburban growth around Martinsboro. Nora's house had been the first to go up in the new section of Mossy Oaks back when she had first moved to Martinsboro midway through eighth grade. The other houses around hers were nice, large affairs, but they suffered from an inherent red brick plainness. They were rubber-stamped, gabled, brick, boxy behemoths with small windows and even smaller, efficient, yards. Nora's house was an elegant Cape Cod-ish throwback with the charm grown into its cedar shingle roof, and wood siding painted a pure white.

Mossy Oaks had few old oaks left and was in fact more densely populated by tall longleaf pine trees, cones dotted about below them, and a few remaining broad elms. Most people knew the neighborhood as The Pines. The Pines was on the sprawling fringes of Martinsboro, outside the city limits and home to the more middle-class students of Liberty High. Here, the sons and daughters of professionals—business owners, teachers, lawyers, financial planners, and engineers—enjoyed the American dream. The families of The Pines were mostly just beginning to find success in their jobs and careers.

Nora thought about what to wear as she walked through the house—it all depended on what she and Augustus were going to do that day. Feeling satisfied, she flopped down onto the living room sofa. A breeze blew through, the leaves of the tree outside the window stirred, and the clock continued to tick. Being full of spring morning energy, she got up and went over to the stereo and began looking through her mother's CDs. She was expecting Augustus to arrive at any moment. A surge of panic caused her to put the CDs down and go look in the driveway for his car. She had lately begun to worry as Augustus's behavior had become increasingly odd—again. He would disappear for long stretches; not call or not return calls, not be where he said he was going to be. He was exhausted and short-tempered all the time. In spite of all this, she loved him, was willing to support him through whatever it was. Augustus was not the only thought occupying her mind on this morning.

Her birthday was next week and was the only real time she had to face one important point of her existence: Nora had been adopted. Her parents had told her at a young age, thinking it best. This fact had surreptitiously attached itself, subconsciously, to every thought she had. She didn't know who she was or where she came from. The parents she knew had adopted her a couple of weeks after she had been born. A sadness was always there when she looked at the two people who loved her most and didn't see anything of herself looking back. At times she even resented their truthfulness and wondered if she would have figured the truth on her own. Yes—the nagging feeling of something just not being right had always been there, even after she had understood as best she could. It was bothering her more and more, recently.

As the years had gone by, Nora had grown up in a way that is extremely rare; her parents were like good stepparents, with a loving, objective calmness and acceptance. Her parents had always treated her thoughtfully, they were mindful of her feelings and personality—always knowing that her experience would be different from their own. She was never taken for granted or used as a pawn like so many genetic offspring are. Frustrations were never taken out on her. They were liberal with her, and she was no doubt freer than the typical teenager and resented it. As an only child she would never be subjected to the pressure to emulate or carry some family burden. Her future had no DNA to map it and, most alarming, no guide other than love to lead her. The only thing thicker than blood is irony, and her life would be one of revelation.

Frenzied and desperately needing sleep, Augustus was taking his usual route through The Pines on a normal, sparkling day. He always drove past the houses of his friends first to see if they were home. Since he and Nora had gotten back together it made him feel a part of the group again. Everybody lived in The Pines—everybody. For the past four years The Pines had been his adopted home. He had sped through its suburban landscape on gravel-colored unmarked streets in the moonlight of the summer and the numb cold of winter. For Augustus, The Pines was a refuge where he could feel disentangled, anonymous on the road, smile at the beauty of the day, or feel closer to the edge of some ruined dream. Augustus had assumed all families were like his and had been shocked, often appalled, when the workings of other families were revealed to him. He lived in a large older house one block from Coxville's downtown. His family had been there for generations, and he felt a rootedness that was alien to the transient nature of his friends' houses. His house had vast, high-ceilinged rooms, but it was creaky, felt worn, and was to Augustus not as nice as the newly built homes in The Pines. Why his mother and father lived there confused him. He attributed it to his father's stinginess and the fact that Hart was rarely at home.

Tripp's house, dark blue, hidden in a forest of trees, came first in the neighborhood. His car was there in its usual spot next to the basketball goal. Next was Frank's house, white and plain with a treeless yard in a dipped curve. His car was gone. Then Augustus took a left on Irvine and rode past Virginia's house—a graduate from last year who had gone on to college—and waved at her dad raking in the yard. The neighborhood had not calmed him. Augustus felt nauseated by the lack of activity and troubled by the thought of the upcoming weekend, the chaos of Junior/Senior weekend. There was only one thing that had to be done first.

Augustus pulled into Nora's driveway, behind her car, recalling a day he and Nora had spent at the beach the previous summer.

"Go to the coast and stand just where the water rolls over into white foam and from that earthly ledge—land meeting water—look to that other edge where the sky rests on the horizon." She recited from memory, something she had written and shown him in a notebook.

"Hold your arm out and point with your finger and try to follow the line. Do you think you could have made it so straight?"

Augustus got out of his car, walked the pathway he knew so well, and climbed the steps. The first time he had ever been there—it been in the winter—was their first date, a double date, the one where Tripp droved his father's minivan because Augustus didn't have his license yet. The foursome had gone to downtown Martinsboro, to the Town Commons, so Tripp and Betty could make out, and he and Nora had stayed in the car. Nora, not having a license either, decided to drive anyway, so they took the minivan cruising. Her gall to drive without a license awed him.

He stopped at the door to watch an approaching car. He heard first the low squawking of pop music. It was a small four-door car that Augustus recognized from school. There were four girls in it who he had seen at school but did not know. Sophomores. They were right in front of him now, the music blaring, the small car leaning as they rounded the curve in front of Nora's house. There was an intense conversation going on, their voices carrying, and he saw that the driver was laughing hysterically at something. He wondered what it was like for them in that car. It made him shudder.

They were young new drivers, possibly one of them didn't have a license at all and was feeling the most adventuresome. Augustus thought about those first few months of freedom, remembering the world feeling expansive and magical. Martinsboro had seemed so large back then. The days were short and riotous. In an uproar to go places you had never been, meet people you had never met.

The girls did not see him there on the porch as they passed. Augustus turned to the door and knocked and, when he got no answer, he opened it and went in.

"Nora!" he called out.

"In here."

Augustus went toward the living room. She was standing at the bookcase and turned to him, haltingly, and, after a look, they hugged each other slightly.

Nora was alarmed. She could see from his red eyes that he needed sleep. He was wearing the same thing he had had on the previous night and it looked like he had slept in it.

"Are you alright?" she asked.

"I'm fine."

"Are you sure you're alright," she asked? "Did you go out after you left here?"

"No. Why do you ask?" he said, trying not to look at her.

"You look like shit, go take a shower."

When her suggestion bounced off the coma-like gaze of Augustus, she knew something was terribly wrong. Augustus was staring out the window. He put his hand down on the couch. Tried to remain silent for one more minute. He still wanted her so much, but he couldn't keep his mind off what he had to do. He would fight it, hold out another day if he could, another sleepless night. If he was so incapable of controlling his thoughts, he would never be able to do anything but hurt her. His mind drifted. Would his mother and father be angry and cast that all-too-familiar disapproving look and tone of voice on him when he told them what he'd done again?

Augustus turned, clasped his hands behind his head and looked at Nora, who had now sat down.

"What do you want to do today?" he asked.

"I don't know, I just feel so lazy," she said, reaching out for him to come over to her.

He stood, immoveable and blank. Nora sighed.

"Then let's talk about my birthday. We could go over all the things you're going to get me for being the best girlfriend in the world."

"Humph!"

"I'm not the best girlfriend in the world?"

"You're okay. Nothing special."

Nora frowned, then tried to recover.

"Are my presents in the car? I bet they are!" She got up to go see.

Augustus stood and stopped her.

He went and stood in front of the French doors, looking far off, as Nora sat back.

"Why did you leave last night?" she asked.

"I needed some sleep."

"Then why do you look so tired? What did you guys do last night?"

"I told you I went home."

"You could have slept here."

"It's not the same. I don't sleep well here when your parents are out of town. I keep expecting to wake up and find them standing over me."

"Even though you knew I would be here alone."

He sat on the end of the couch

"You just don't give a shit," Nora muttered.

"What does that mean?" he asked.

"You know I always get sad around my birthday."

"Then fucking do something about it."

"What the fuck is that supposed to mean?"

"You know what it means. Find out who your real parents are."

"No. I won't."

"Why?"

"My parents would feel bad."

"You don't think your parents went into this whole thing not knowing that it would have to be done some day? For God's sake, I can't believe they're not encouraging you."

"So now it's my parents' fault?"

"It doesn't matter whose fault it is. That information is your right and your responsibility."

"My real parents don't deserve me."

Augustus had always wondered what her biological parents looked like. As beautiful as Nora was, he figured they had to be successful, happy people and he just couldn't imagine why they'd had to give her up. Augustus thought his interest in them selfish; it was a mystery that, if discovered, he believed would be for the best, it could be the key to his and Nora's relationship. He didn't think he could live without knowing. He wanted to know more than she did—it frustrated him.

She went outside and sat in the porch swing. Something deep down inside her told her that there was truth in what Augustus suggested and she was just too afraid of being hurt again. Augustus went outside and stood, too angry to sit, but he didn't look at her, he couldn't look at her because if he did, he would love her again.

"What are you looking at?"

Augustus didn't hear her, nor did he move.

"Augustus. For God's sake, please look at me."

He would not face her or let her see, if she could see at all, or know, or feel the pain. He knew he should just do it, but he stopped. Could he do it to her again, especially over something unfair? When he was with her things were better and he could hold them back, but then in a collapse of hope he just couldn't help himself anymore. He lost control.

He imagined her, in a room, a bed, with a person not him. It's a dirty, ugly, cruel place, the mind's imagination. The thought of her being with someone else, the intimacy, little details shared. The betrayal was his. It flooded his mind a thousand times over in the day and night hours and the brutal, most unimaginably difficult truth, was that he could blame only himself. Augustus was overwhelmed with guilt. The only thing to do was to separate himself from her again and the thoughts would fade.

"Augustus, look at me, please tell me what's wrong. I know something is wrong, last night it was like you were on some other planet again. You know prom is next week but you won't even talk about it."

"I can't live like this!" Augustus turned and shouted at her. "I don't know what's wrong! My head. It hurts all the time like a headache, but there's nothing wrong, the thoughts in my head are hurting. God, does that make any sense? I know I'm hurting you being this way, I'm hurting everyone, but it won't stop. I don't know how to make it stop!"

"What's bothering you so much?" Nora asked.

"Everything. This shitty world. My father. My mother. Take your pick. The fucking people we know. The fucking knee-deep bullshit surrounding everything. I keep asking myself why."

"Why what?" Nora asked

An iron gloom was in Augustus's face. His determination iced over, and rage swept through his eyes. He wanted to be released.

"Why? What do you mean 'why'? It's the 'why' that overshadows everything, all the time."

He dropped to his knees in front of her and put his hands on the hands he loved so much, but they felt like someone else's hands, and he wanted them to feel like hers again. He was grotesquely pleading now. Nora, disoriented, recoiled from him, seeing desperation. She was horrified.

"Why did I break up with you? Please tell me. Explain it to me. Why would I do it? How could I do? Why would a person do such a thing? Why did I make everything so awful? And why did you then do …"

Nora straightened up, her own resolve gripping her, miserable with disbelief.

"You did the same fucking things. You fucking asshole. You moved on. How can you even bring it up? You know how it makes me feel. What you did was worse. I fucking loved you and you fucking dumped me. Don't you remember me begging you not to? I was in love with you! I would have done anything for you. You had to have more of whatever it was you wanted. I can't believe this. Why do we keep talking about the same fucking bullshit over and over? Get over it, you selfish asshole. Why am I so stupid to keep believing in your bullshit?"

Disgusted, she got up and moved away from him. Augustus was still kneeling. Confused, he struggled to stand. He knew, with a bizarre sensation of a void in his mind, that there was no answer to his questions. He wanted to scream. Nora looked at him coldly.

"You're going to bring up Jake now, aren't you?" Nora said. "I can't fucking believe you. So do you want to hear it again. You're so sick sometimes."

The name came searing into his chest.

"I don't know what to say, Augustus, I can only say I'm sorry, which I shouldn't have to do in the first place."

Augustus and Nora looked at each other with finality.

"I know. I know. I know." Augustus pleaded. "What's wrong with me, what's wrong with me? Why can't I feel happiness? I can't stop."

Nora began to cry. All her strengths, the reasons she loved him, wilted away into hopelessness. She had told him about Jake. She knew now that she should have lied or said nothing, but Augustus had insisted, he thought he wanted the truth, that somehow, mistakenly, it would bring him peace. He had drawn it out of her with promises— promises that were impossible to keep. Part of her wanted him to know, to hurt him in the same way she had been hurt, so he would know that she was desired, that she was valuable and precious. The connection between them, the trust that could be taken for granted and reveled in, was gone. Augustus had taken it badly. He was riddled with guilt; his mind seethed with a vicious jealousy when he should have been happy. The inherent fragility of the mind's peace had become apparent to him. Nora was still grasping something no longer there. She had hoped that his jealousy would subside, waiting for his conscience to find a balance. She looked out the French doors Augustus had gazed out of when he had first arrived, and she now knew what was in his mind and now it was in hers, and she thought about how she just wished she could leave and never come back.

After she had told him, he became worse. He twisted every repulsive, contrived situation in his mind and spun new depths of self-loathing. Nora tried to remain silent. She was helpless as his imagination tormented him. She wished she knew how to make it stop. So she stayed with him, trying to do the best she could. The wonderful flights of fancy they envisioned together were fading among the unfathomable distress each day brought. The moral lining of her life, she thought, was coming undone by a sense of doom. She herself was becoming more withdrawn and callous. They had changed each other, formed each other into something special, new, and different, but now she had to do it again for them. This had always made it worth holding on to and then she would sleep. But she was beginning to lose sleep. Nora sighed deeply.

Augustus turned and looked up at Nora. He didn't recognize her.

"Augustus, I want you to leave and please don't ever… You know what? Fuck it… Please just leave."

Augustus fumbled his way through the kitchen, and went out the door looking back at her. She did not look at him. Nora listened for the door to close then hurried upstairs to her room. She lay down and pulled a pillow to herself tightly. She cried great waves of tears, surprised she had them still in her. Her mind was frozen with pain. And when she couldn't cry anymore, when the pain started to go away and her mind seemed to put everything in perspective and she was finally at ease, she sniffed, dried her eyes on her sleeve, and got up, determined to do something.

She contemplated the next day. She would have to see him. He was everywhere in her life. She would see him, but she would have to ignore him, pretend he wasn't there, and he would have to do the same. She could not get away from him; it was the end of senior year, it was awful to think of all they should have shared. The sense of loss grew as her thoughts moved over the coming months and she could only shake her head. She was suddenly overcome with an intense fear for Augustus; she knew how destructive he could be, and she wouldn't be there for him. In that moment, everything became clear to her. She felt pity. She felt sorry for him. He had everything but, really, he had nothing. She had to let him go. It dawned on her for the first time who Augustus really was, and she shuddered. She rubbed her shaking hands together and held them to her mouth, listening to the rapid beating of her heart. She cried until she could cry no more and fell asleep. And the day was over, and it was night.

Roman woke late, the morning light burned through the window, and he rose from deadness. He had taken Cassandra home at midnight and returned to the dark house to sleep. No one else was up. He crept through the house, saw closed doors, and went into the living room where the strangeness of the house brought a vague horror to his senses. Drew came in without seeing him, went to the refrigerator, took out milk, and drank from the carton. He turned around.

"Didn't see you there. Been up long?"

"Nah, just got up."

"Where's Cassandra?" Drew asked.

"Took her home last night. Came back and crashed."

"Mmhhmm. Did a…. you guys do it?"

"What do you want me to say?"

"That's not an answer."

Roman shook his head.

"Maybe next time. You need a ride?"

The ride home was silent. Drew's coolness was matched only by Roman's contentment. The world looked bright and new to him, closer, more vivid. Drew drove, windows down, and neither of them reached for the radio. Easing down from the buzz of the prom, a car pulled up beside them, heavy bass beating, and they didn't notice. The fast-food joints, strip malls, and streetlights looked propped up and fake, like they were made of cardboard. The wind blew through the open windows and they both lit cigarettes and smoked. Roman thought about Cassandra and where she was at that moment. He saw that moment and then the next and on and on, like looking to the side in those mirrors at department stores, the ones you try on clothes in front of. His future was a movie playing in his head and every moment was his to dream up, his reality to create. This went on for the rest of the ride. Finally, they reached the cul-de-sac where Roman lived and Drew wheeled the car around and parked at the curb. Roman's neighbor was on a lawnmower, grass shooting out the deck and the heavy clanging of the engine. Roman squinted at him in the sunlight.

"Peace out, man," Drew uttered through the window.

"Later," he said, and Drew drove off.

Roman looked up at his house and was overwhelmed by a feeling of sadness for it. He walked up the driveway to the front steps, got his key out, expecting the house to be empty, but the door was unlocked. He did not call out as he entered but he knew his father was somewhere, and he expected to be criticized for not coming home last night. The TV was blank and reflective, and Baron was at the kitchen table, sitting very still, looking out the window above the sink, the one that looked into the small backyard, the one his mother would look out of, watching the birds eat at the feeders she had hung. Roman went in and Baron didn't move. His arms were crossed and he was as still as Roman had ever seen him. Roman sat down in the chair across from him. The emptiness of the house since his mother had left was like a third presence. Roman looked closer at Baron's face and could see that something had happened.

"Your grandfather has died," Baron said suddenly.

"Pop?"

"No. Not your Pop, your other grandfather. My father."

"What did he die of?"

"He died in his sleep. I don't know. Old age, I guess."

"Have I ever met him?"

"When you were little."

Roman was confused.

"He left me a house and your mother is selling this house, so I have to move there. Do you want to live with your mother or me?"

Roman, stunned, wobbled as if standing on a precipice. His mouth opened to say words, but no sound came out. Baron had never mentioned his own father. A vague memory with no name, only a place, formed in his mind. He was reeling. He had been naive enough to take a clumsy step into believing in his dreams. He saw flashes of the life he imagined just minutes ago, about Cassandra, to the furthest brink of his existence and, working backward, they vanished, one magnificent frame at a time.

"We're going home," Baron said.

"Where's home?" Roman asked.

FOUR

Roman looked around the barren house, filled with unpacked boxes. He was alone; the morning was at a dead standstill and the only sound was the ceiling fan whirring overhead. He went out the front door, the wooden screen door slamming behind him, and stood on the porch. From his elevated view he saw a cracked, weather-blackened, narrow concrete walkway. He followed it. Ahead he saw that it led to a two-bay garage on the intersection's corner. Roman stopped; to his right he turned and a blue Ford F-150 rolled slowly to a stop, its driver barely visible, at the stop light. The truck turned left and went into the car lot on the opposite corner. The new cars of the dealership cast a glare in the morning sun. Roman continued on his path, jumped a small ditch, and was in a paved lot. One of the large garage bay doors was open, facing the road, and he heard the sound of a radio playing. The decrepit building and garage loomed on the side of Roman's new house, as if part of it. Next to the garage was the main building. It was square, with cream stucco walls and a red clay tile roof that made it look like it belonged in the desert. There were two large windows facing the street and the entrance was covered by a shelter that extended out to where two relics stood, gas pumps from back when stations were full service. It was a shell of its former self, dusty, worn, untouched. The shiny new oil brands and their glistening new, brightly lit stations were in charge of gas distribution now. They sprang up, built during the night, bustling, money changing hands, cooler doors slamming, people hurrying in and out. Roman went in the old station, noticing the smell of gasoline, acrid solvents, cool steel, and the concrete—blackened, stained, the oil baked in.

Baron, in navy Dickies and a button-down shirt with his name on a patch on the pocket, standing and somehow slouched, took off his green Royster cap and wiped the sweat from his forehead. Roman picked up an air wrench and pulled the trigger. The air compressed gun let out its shrill warbling sound. He pulled the trigger again, then put it down. Roman saw Baron disappear behind the raised hood of a car. He went up to the car.

"You startled me," Baron said, reaching into the motor. "Can you hand me a wrench?"

"Which one?"

"Nine-sixteenths."

Roman surveyed the tools scattered around on the concrete floor, the worktable, and the drawers of the toolbox for the wrench his father needed. After all these years he still couldn't recognize a wrench by looking at it as his father could, so each one he picked up required him to look for the small indicator numbers.

"What are you doing?" Baron asked impatiently from beneath the hood.

"Looking for it," Roman answered quickly.

He found the wrench and put it in his father's outstretched hand. By Roman's feet was a rolling cart he had been so fascinated with when he was younger and smaller, when he would use it as a skateboard and push himself around the garage as his father worked.

Roman looked down at his father's stained pants and thought about how much he hated grease. He looked at his own hands to make sure he hadn't gotten any on them. It was inevitable in a garage. His mother, he remembered, hated grease too. His father's hands had always seemed to be permanently stained a darker shade throughout Roman's life. It had always embarrassed him. Baron had gone months without working and still his hands were stained. Roman wouldn't look at them.

He thought about how tidy his mother was and how she always smelled of fabric softener and always seemed to be busy about the house cooking, or making something for the holidays, or painting in the dining room. Organizing, she claimed, was her only virtue. He missed her and wondered if his parents had loved each other. He always felt that his father was lucky because his mother had taken a tender pity on him and married him—and now she wasn't taking pity on him anymore.

That morning Roman had arisen early and in the same foul mood that had been getting progressively worse throughout each new day in the sleepy ruralness of Coxville. He had spent his first Friday night in Coxville at home, a vacant loneliness in his thoughts, watching TV with his father downstairs. They could still do that, watch a ball game together, but, feeling the need to be alone with his thoughts, he went to the strange, empty room he now occupied. He looked through his yearbook for awhile then closed it and lay on his back staring at the ceiling, his mind turning over recent events and his life back in Seaside.

When he went to bed, he had trouble sleeping. He kept reliving random sentiments, impressions of awe, and a specific anger at the world. Half awake, haphazard memories would swirl in his mind and cause a smile before he drifted off. There was the time he and Miles were caught by the police with a back seat full of mailboxes.

"What in the hell are you kids doing with all those mailboxes?" the officer had asked. He and Miles had looked at one another and shrugged, not really knowing. Having to take them all back, facing the people he had wronged, having to apologize, was agonizing.

What he missed most now was the sense of unlocking the secret places of his Seaside world. Here before him was a whole new riddle, this new future made his mind wince. The music was the same, familiar songs attached to memories brought back the past, as usual. Miles and Drew, he knew, would be somewhere trying to outdo each other; he could hear their laughter, as if it were coming from a far-off summer night. He, Miles, and Drew had the same sense of sarcastic humor forged from earlier days spent together, pregirlfriends, before they could drive. They were his best friends, but he had always felt a nagging suspicion that they regarded him as an outsider. Last summer he had spent most of his time with a different crew who liked to surf. Miles and Drew, not catching the surfing bug, had shrugged and gone their own way.

Roman remembered awkward moments, too many to count, embarrassments and fumbled crushes. He closed his eyes and saw an ethereal procession of girls who had sparked his interest, who had radiated a wispy calmness, who had changed him through the intricacies of their personalities. And he, like everyone, believed in the innocent impulse, the one in everyone's young heart, for simplicity, for the ease of love, for the one guy and one girl—forever.

Roman, considering self-awareness a virtue, figured he had a pretty good idea about what was going on back in Seaside. He was popular, in a conventional way, was an established figure, not having made any real waves, and by usually having a girlfriend he had stayed away from some of the weirder stories he had heard. He was well-liked. He realized now he had become lethargic, comfortable, docile, and had devolved into the oblivion of a fixture, in one word—boring. He realized that, in his blasé state he had cheated his real self, the one that aspired to greatness, and precious time had been squandered. It must have been what the Cassandra thing was all about. Maybe that's why he had gone so quietly.

In the past week he had also noticed a considerable difference in the various characters of Liberty High School and those back at Laney. Liberty High, built in 1970, right after desegregation, had no real history; it was a factory, a boxy, pale brown brick monolith surrounded by a black parking lot, next to a sprawling sports complex—track, football field, baseball field, softball field, soccer field, tennis courts, and field house. Still, Liberty was a lively hub of shuffling, heavy backpack-laden aspiring careerists. The student parking lot, to the far right beside the gymnasium, was filled with a kaleidoscopic assortment of vehicles—small cars, big cars, old cars, trucks, really big, tired trucks, low riders, heaps, clunkers—you name it. The burnt orange buses were opposite, on the other side of the school, beside the cafeteria, in no-man's-land. Roman had never been there. The school was ten miles outside of Coxville on Worthington Road and was surrounded by stray water oaks, strips of pine trees, old tobacco barns, and neatly squared farmland, in the middle of nowhere. The smell of sweat and ammonia circulated down the locker-lined connecting halls and produced a most unpleasant aroma to which the students and teachers had become immune. Only the visitor would walk in the front door and ask, "What is that smell?"

Liberty was tinged with a universal cruelty, stark differences, an obviousness of class, and a seething, unspoken jealousy when its corridors were filled with the bobbing bookbags and languorous footfalls. His first week at Liberty he was an observer, a pathfinder, enjoying the anonymity, the inquiring sideways glances, the people talking around him in conspiratorial, hushed voices. And the girls—they loved a new guy. Their curious eyes filled him with a sudden pride, and he held in a smile. The students were in summer wear; sandals, flip-flops, deck shoes, shorts, T-shirts, polos, sundresses, skirts, and halter tops despite the industrial air freezing them in the classrooms, the metal desks cold to the touch. There had been the awkward moment during the roll call in every class where the usual routine had been broken by his arrival. They waited to hear the intruder speak. He wandered the new halls, the classrooms, and parking lot with a cool detachment, his gaze suspicious, alone and confident at the same time. A few curious, somewhat odd, wayward people had started conversations with him, people like him maybe, new, with few friends. He had been cordial and friendly.

Back in Seaside, at Laney, it was mostly affluent suburban kids, homogenized, with an air of entitlement. The major separation was along lines of purported indifference. Roman was considered poor there, but his mother had a high-profile job, was a bit of a local minor celebrity, a TV news personality, and incredibly attractive. At Liberty, he noticed a wider variety of kids—from the rural working class, country boys, rednecks, and inner-city kids shipped in from Martinsboro. The few rich kids he noticed tended to stick together, often in twos and threes. He had not met any, but he had overheard conversation about people who went to the school's rival, Scott High. Still, there was a tension at Liberty that made him uneasy and nervous, like some naive freshman.

He sometimes regretted not putting up a fight against the move and going so quietly. Concern for his father, a melancholic hopelessness, and an outright fear of confrontation had weakened the reality of what was happening. The news had come so fast and, with his mother's leaving still looming in his and his father's mind, it was more than either could fully grasp. He just went with it—stunned—and simply put one foot in front of the other. Roman and his father now lived in a small, old house next to the main intersection through Coxville. It was much smaller than the Californian ranch-style home they had lived in in one of Seaside's new subdivisions.

Roman wasn't impressed with the new house. "Does it have air conditioning?" he asked.

"Sure," Baron said, and pointed to a mildewed square box in one of the windows.

The new house was one story, with three bedrooms off a small hall that made them almost a part of the kitchen and living room. The floors were hardwood, dull and scuffed, the walls some an off-white hue, some with peeling wallpaper. Upon looking at the place for the first time, Roman had barely been able to control his disbelief. The house in Seaside, while small but respectable, had been decorated primarily with his mother's élan, which had given the place a pleasant warmth. This house, with its sagging floors and rusty pipes, gave Roman a sinking feeling. Its only reasonably quaint attributes were the two fireplaces on either side of the house, one which served the living room and the other both bedrooms.

"Can we build fires in the winter?" Roman had asked.

"You'll have to chop the wood," Baron responded.

Roman and his father had only moved a few things in, the necessities; a kitchen table, microwave, sofa, recliner, and TV in the living room. In the bedrooms, mattresses and bureaus only. When Roman had asked his father what was going to happen to the rest of their stuff, his mother's stuff, and the house in Seaside, Baron had only told him not to worry about it and that he was having everything moved here later.

"Why are we here?" Roman remembered asking when he just couldn't go without knowing any longer, after he felt he had quietly cooperated with the move, proven himself dutiful and loyal. Surely, after that he deserved an answer. Baron had no answer and just stared at the road as he drove, gripping the steering wheel, words almost forming on his lips. Roman let it go. It didn't take long to move in the few things they had brought, then he and his father sat side by side on the steps of the front porch, sweating, sharing the same glass of water. Roman looked out at a new town and a new life, and he looked over at his father and saw that Baron's eyes moved over what was before them and he got the feeling that his father had been there before.

Baron had shut down his shop in Seaside and moved his two most cherished items here, his tools and his car. The car now sat under a heavy tarp in the back corner of the garage. Baron had been hanging around in there for the past week, usually when Roman was at school, poking around, moving this and that. No sign had been hung nor any grand opening announced, but someone was there, the open bay doors said so.

Roman went back and sat on the stool beside the car, looking out the garage bay door into the beautiful spring day and watched the stoplight flash its eternal yellow. The flashing red faced the traffic coming from Martinsboro. There was a university there, he knew, where there were wild, hedonistic debaucheries of the sort high schoolers dream of.

His father's silence, detachment, and strange behavior still worried him. He tried to understand what his father was going through, but most of the time he just tried not to think about it. They rarely spoke or acknowledged one another, except for when he needed money for gas or to go out to eat. He thought about Cassandra mostly, and what he was going to do now, in this small hick town, and how he could get back to Seaside after he graduated. He missed the beach, the wind blowing off the ocean at night, and the short trip it took to get to the ocean. The smell of Coxville was different. It smelled like gasoline instead of the rotting fish and saltwater smell of the coast.

Roman and Baron both turned as a Dodge Caravan pulled up. A figure with dark hair and a big smile appeared from the vehicle and started to walk up to the garage as if he had done so hundreds of times before. Baron, recognizing the visitor, went quickly out to greet him.

"Gino! It's good to see you," Baron said with a rare enthusiasm and smile, as he wiped his hands.

"Baron. I wondered when you'd come back to town."

"I remember the last time I saw you," Baron said.

"John's wedding."

"That was ten years ago."

"You haven't changed a bit. It's been too long."

"Yeah, too long. Too long," Baron mumbled, more to himself than to the visitor. "So, what are you doing now? You and Vanessa still together?" he added.

"Yeah, I'm still teaching at the high school."

"The one here?" Baron said, pointing with his finger, indicating Coxville.

Gino nodded yes. "Got three kids."

"That's great, Gino."

"Thanks."

"What are you teaching?"

"English, can you believe it?"

"So, you're a family man. How old are they?"

"One's a freshman in college, one's in high school, and the youngest in middle school."

"You didn't name one of them Gino, Jr., did you?"

"As a matter of fact, I did."

"You want a drink or something? Come on in."

Gino followed Baron into the bay. He saw Roman and nodded. "Who's this?" he asked.

"Oh, sorry, Gino, this is my son, Roman."

"How are you?" Gino asked, offering his hand.

"Hello," Roman said shaking the visitor's hand. Roman politely excused himself and went out of the garage but stopped nearby so he could listen.

"What are you working on?" Gino asked.

"Just messing around with this car Tom Sheppard brought in," Baron said, handing Gino a canned drink from the refrigerator.

"I didn't see you at the funeral," Gino said.

"I couldn't get back."

"Oh," Gino said, looking off and thinking hard what to say. "He was a good man, Baron."

Baron nodded.

"Anyway, I just wanted to stop by, I saw the door open and wanted to say hello. Is Ann here?"

"No." Baron paused. "She's in Seaside."

"Oh."

At the mention of his mother, Roman was disturbed. He decided to leave and walked toward the sidewalk. At the front door he stopped and turned to see the stranger and his father still talking. His father looked happy. Unnoticed, a white convertible Corvette cruised through the intersection; Roman was too distracted to notice it.

On the way home from Nora's Augustus tried to tell himself that he had done the right thing. He took a deep breath and exhaled as he went through the Coxville intersection. The melancholy thoughts were already dissipating and the knot in his stomach loosened. He took another deep breath and wondered why he had tortured himself for so long. Augustus tried to imagine a universe out there in which he and Nora were together.

The guilt, too, was gone, the recurring punishment he forced on himself for the mistake he couldn't live with. It had really been he who was torturing her. The word torture, why torture? It was a bit severe, he thought.

If he could just assign blame confidently, he might have been able to make it work. If he could have broken the endless circles of thought. There was some aspect of the hurt that he could not process. If he'd slept on it maybe things would have been different? He began to feel tired.

Wasn't it she who, in the first place, felt that nothing was ever good enough for her? Wasn't it she who was always starved for attention? Always in the early days of their relationship she repeated "you never" and "why don't you ever." She had driven him away and, in the strangest of ironies, he almost laughed. It was true, in the beginning, he hadn't cared as much as he should have, took things for granted even, broke her heart and learned what it truly meant to love someone. And now he figured he cared too much, and in a warped misplaced fashion. He'd learned the hard way. His own naivete had blinded him to information he'd needed until the situation was beyond control. Augustus felt himself untethered, something dangerous. He had to be extra careful from here on out, even more so than before. He had thought of nothing else except for Nora for the last three years and, oddly enough, it hadn't helped at all. His intense attraction to her only brought them both pain. He decided not to think about her, not to have any contact with her.

"When it goes bad, it just goes bad sometimes," someone had once told him. There was no explaining it. He would miss her, but he figured he had learned everything there was to learn from her. She and her fantasies had brought them to ruin. Nora had ignited his imagination so many years before and now it burned brighter than ever, and he wondered why he had wanted so badly to stay with her. Her absolute confidence and energy had been an aphrodisiac.

He now had to focus. He felt a strange relief as he planned his future. In the past he had always gone back because he got bored. He would find the right girl this time. There had to be someone out there. Someone different, so he would never crave Nora's company again.

After all, he could have any girl he wanted from the way people talked, sometimes even to his face. The condescension in every voice, the resentment in every eye. "You just get all the girls," "He's so-and-so's son," "His father owns that place…," "So, you think you'll hit as many home runs at State next year?" "You got it made."

Augustus gripped the wheel, his knuckles turning white. He turned in, parked, and hurried inside the house.

"Augustus, is that you?" his mother called to him.

He didn't say anything, trying not to be seen on his way up to his room.

"There's some mail for you on the table. I think it's from State. Augustus. Augustus!"

"I heard you," he yelled, and slammed his door.

Hart pulled into the driveway behind Augustus' car and cast a weary glance at it. He hurried up the steps and into the house, passing his wife on the couch. He knew if she saw him, she would see the pent-up anger in his shoulders and stop him.

Hart wanted to calm down, but he couldn't. He went up the stairs, to Augustus's door, and knocked.

"Augustus?" No answer. "Augustus, open this door right now."

He heard movement, felt some trepidation, then the door opened slowly. Augustus held the door open and stood firm, ready for an argument that he was aching to release on someone. Hart stood opposite him, in a similar rage, his jaw clenched.

Augustus turned, hoping at the last minute to avoid the unavoidable. He sat at his desk and started to put his stereo headphones on, as if obeying one command might somehow disperse the tension, when his father came in, snatched the headphones out of his hand, and threw them on the floor.

"Look at me when I'm talking to you," he burst out in a tone Augustus knew well, the high-pitched sound of reproach.

Augustus spun around and stood up, startled, and they looked at each other as if they were strangers. They had both changed into something less than they should have been.

"Where were you today?" Hart demanded.

"Just around," Augustus uttered quietly, not at all ready for what was coming, having forgotten that he said he would be at the lot at eight.

"Around where? What is so important that you just decide you don't have to work?"

"Tripp's house," he said, lying.

"What are you doing at Tripp's house? You were supposed to be at work today at eight."

"Who said?"

"You did. I waited for you all morning. I had things that needed to be done. I have to be able to count on you. If you want things, you have to work for them."

"I'm sick of having this conversation over and over again."

"So am I. Just do what you're told."

"No one else is working," Augustus said offhandedly.

"You're not everyone else. Everyone else can go to the dogs, for all I care. You're supposed to be at the lot after school and on Saturdays."

"Can't I get a day off sometimes? I'm about to graduate. I want to hang out with my friends before everyone leaves. I did your stupid baseball and football and worked in the winter during basketball all year."

"You're still supposed to work. You don't get time off. You have insurance to pay for and the car. We can't keep giving you money for nothing, it's not fair to us."

"I don't want those things. Those are things I never asked for. And besides, you never pay me what you owe me. I'm going to get a job somewhere else. I hate working for you. It's never enough. I can never do anything for you fast enough or right."

"What are you talking about? You get paid more than I could hire someone else for. I pay you for the hours you work."

"I don't feel well," Augustus said, confessing, saying something actually true.

"What do you mean you don't feel well? It's because you're drinking. You look like crap. You need a haircut. Only a sorry, worthless person goes out and drinks," Hart thundered, the room seemingly shaking.

His father hated drinking. He had never seen his father, mother, or anyone in his family drink. The accusations burned in his mind with a ferocity.

"What are you talking about?" Augustus said.

"Don't speak to me like that."

They were yelling at each other now and looking idiotic, ashamed but unable to end it.

Hart took a step toward Augustus and for a moment Augustus thought this was it, but Hart turned.

"Either be at the lot Monday or leave your car keys on the counter," he said as he left the room.

Augustus, humiliated, furious at himself for forgetting and embarrassed about the things he had said, slammed the door behind Hart. Relieved but still smoldering, he locked the door. He hated everything with a seething viciousness. His mind was enveloped in a blazing blackness, vast and opaque, the chasm swallowed him, he knew nothing and saw nothing, he embraced it, and suddenly, he was asleep, for the first time in three nights.

FIVE

Roman, acutely conscious of the dreadful slowness of time, stopped to glare, with malice, at the clock. He realized he had been pacing, and when he started up again, he heard the floor creaking beneath his steps. He went over to the window again and looked out, adjusting the blinds, pulling one up and letting it down for no real reason, but there was still nothing to see except the same yard, the same trees, and the same road, unchanged. He was anxious. Junior/Senior weekend was here, and he was already late for it. Earlier in the week he had told Baron the coming weekend was Junior/Senior and waited for a response but, as usual, Baron was distracted and only grunted unintelligibly with his mouth full of a chocolate chip cookie.

Roman, wearing his red bathing suit and a white T-shirt, sat down on the leather recliner, kicking it out. He put his hands behind his head and stared up at the ceiling, trying not to notice the cobwebs, and took a deep breath, trying to relax. Almost immediately, hearing a car on the road, he sprang from the chair, went out onto the porch, and watched a car, not the one he was looking for, approach the intersection. It came to a stop then started up again breaking the town's still, lazy aura.

Roman pondered the approaching release from rule, from restraints. He decided, and it was final, he would abandon himself, his caution. He would be someone else. At Liberty his newness was waning, Junior/Senior overtaking all else, pervading the hushed halls, hanging like an apocalyptic prophesy. The school week had been calm, students suspiciously attentive. Roman listened as his new friends, recalled stories on the back porches and in the driveways of The Pines. Surely, they were exaggerated, he thought, but in them was some hint of truth, and slowly he started to understand, here on the brink of it—this was no ordinary weekend. He suddenly felt a warm radiance, having never really been away, alone, on his own, and now he was about to go two full nights that would be totally different from any he had ever known. There would be no time for sleep.

Roman had never really had a curfew for the last two years, thanks to his father's permissiveness, and had tended to come home early, to avoid worrying him. He had snuck out of the house on occasion. Still, those were constraints. There was always staying over at the friend's house whose parents were out of town. That had been fun, except for the fear of being caught or the friend's parents coming home at some incredible embarrassing moment. This was different. They would be away from any threat of interruption. Total privacy and freedom for two nights and a day. He counted the hours he would have. How had it not occurred to him until now? He had thought very little about the world beyond high school, when he would be out on his own. No one to answer to every minute of every day. This briefly worried him because he remembered how people tended to lose control. He just knew that it was going to be one hell of a good time, no matter what happened.

Where was Tripp? Tripp had the trunk load of beer. In minutes he would be on his way to join the five other high schools; Liberty, Scott, Maraschino, Farmington, and Fulton. Every high school student in Catechna County, massing at beach house rented by older brother, Aunt So-And-So's condo, motels, campers, tents, all at the same beach on the same weekend. A whole small beach town invaded, which meant even more new people to meet—novel, unknown girls, and all of it—theirs for a weekend.

Tripp's beater, a 1983 champagne-colored Honda Accord, turned into the drive. Roman rushed for the front door and went out, the door slamming behind him.

"They kept me an extra hour at the airport. Fucking community service. Don't worry, man. We'll get down there in plenty of time."

Tripp was narrowly built, the same height as Roman, with wide blue eyes, flopping blond hair glinting in the sun, fair skin, wearing a white Budweiser T-shirt and black swim trunks and, of course, shoeless. Tripp was always barefoot, going through a shoe-hating period, scorning all, as he saw it, of modernity's unnecessary comforts.

"Have you talked to anyone down there?" Roman asked.

"A few people," Tripp said, holding up a piece of paper. "I've got phone numbers and directions to everyone's places."

Roman placed his bag in the back seat beside the cooler. They both got into the car, put their sunglasses on, and pulled out. Tripp raced the small car's engine and shifted the stick into second. Roman leaned his seat back and lit a cigarette as a calmness finally descended before the storm. The car stopped at the intersection in front of Roman's house. They took a right and Roman looked back at the garage, its crumbling facade in contrast to the new dealership across the way, and he felt a tinge of pity for his father. For now, Roman put it out of his mind—there were things to do. In the side mirror he watched his corner of town as it became smaller and smaller as they pulled away. He looked at the passing glass facades and felt the car humming down Main Street in Coxville until the sidewalks were no more, and the large mossy oak trees, and the well-landscaped, aged, ornate houses, leaving behind the quaint, sleepy bedroom community vibe as they headed out of Coxville. They passed the green and white city limits sign and sped up, the newly planted fields rippling past them. Tripp held the wheel with one hand at 12 o'clock and smoked with the other.

"What went on down there last night?" Roman asked him.

"Not much, they told me they just sat around the house and drank. They said they got fucked up too early and couldn't make it out. I heard Scott had a rager. At Logan's place. His parents have a monster house right on the beach. It's at the other end of the island but I'm sure we'll get down there tonight or tomorrow night. It's not as big as Augustus's beach house, but it's big."

Roman had lived at the beach and had been in many of his friends' colossal beach houses, always with awe and amazement, but never one that would be without prying parents. He closed his eyes for a moment, magnificent mansions in his mind, the wind blowing in the open windows, as they crossed the Catechna County line.

"The only thing we have to worry about is roadblocks," Tripp said gravely.

Roman thought about the cases of beer in the trunk and eyed the cooler in the back seat unenthusiastically.

"Roadblocks?" he asked.

"Yeah, it's the great myth of Junior/Senior," Tripp said, flipping through the radio stations.

"That's the dumbest thing I've ever heard," Roman replied.

"I know, but the theory is that the cops set up roadblocks at the bridge to catch underage people drinking on the way down to the beach with carloads of beer."

"The cops don't know it's Junior/Senior."

"They know it's Memorial Day weekend."

"Roadblocks are at night."

"I know, it's just that people always talk about it, so everyone gets it into their head and worries about it."

"Do you really think there'll be roadblocks?"

"All I know is, if there are," Tripp said as he reached back, lifted the lid to the cooler, scooped two beers out of the ice, handed one to Roman, cracked one open for himself, and took a huge gulp, "we're fucked."

They laughed.

"Fuck it," Roman affirmed.

Roman took sips from his beer covertly whenever there wasn't any traffic behind them or oncoming. He visualized the narrow sandy streets, sand dunes, desert-like grasses, hanging wet towels, curious architecture, cedar shingles, stilted houses holding inexplicable secrets, the harsh salty wind. He could hear the sound of ice sloshing in the back seat as they passed a car. There would be an endless supply of beer, for sure, and Roman tasted the bitterness, the malty coldness, as he drank.

At first, they said little as the sun beat down on the windshield. They were barefoot, sweat beading on their foreheads, the constant wind the only sound. They passed an endless parade of barns and farmhouses. They had the windows rolled down and beers between their legs. Tripp was doing 65; Roman's job was to look out for state troopers.

"How far is it?" Roman asked.

Tripp thought for a minute and looked at the can in his hand. "About six beers."

"No, really."

" 'Bout an hour and 15, but there'll probably be traffic."

Roman took over the radio while Tripp smoked and drank and flipped through radio stations. He lit a cigarette with the car lighter and thought how it was the first hot day of May and wondered if the ocean would be warm. It was a day telling you summer was coming, when the only thing really to think about was the pool or the ocean. It was around 88 degrees or so, he figured. At that moment he realized that he had forgotten something essential—his surfboard. It was in the backyard shed. Maybe someone else would have one, he hoped. Some really good waves would be nice.

He watched the oncoming traffic zoom past them and then followed the ditches and power lines, anything to make the time go by faster. Tripp took out a joint and they smoked it. They passed through a small town, people walking, sitting on porches, going into stores, going about their business, oblivious to the grand events at hand. Tripp turned left at a stoplight and they headed back out, passing a state trooper with someone pulled over. Both were worried for a moment, but then they were back out in the green, rural, isolation. Roman was in unknown territory now. It was all new. Traffic became heavier and every chance Tripp got he dropped down into fourth gear, full of contempt, and punched the gas to fly around family filled minivans, tractor-trailers, beaters, trucks, and all speed limit obeyers. On the open roads they could drink without worries. Then, passing through the city of Haven, they had to keep their beers down and were stopped in traffic waiting for an old bridge over the river to close.

"It's straight on from here," Tripp said.

"How far?"

"Not far."

Roman thought about the roadblocks. He tried to clear his mind, to think nothing.

"Where are we going to stay?" Roman inquired offhandedly, trying to sound as if he didn't care, when he really did.

"There are lots of places we can crash," Tripp said, hoping to ease his friend's mind.

The word "crash" worried Roman; he would feel much better knowing they had a bed and a place to stay.

"Relax, man!" Tripp said, reaching over and slapping Roman on the shoulder. "Not knowing where we're going to stay is part of the fun. We're like drifters, vagabonds. Going where the fates take us."

"Fates, yeah. You mean bums?" laughed Roman.

"Don't worry about it. Everyone thinks you're cool. We can stay at Augustus's house. He's got plenty of room. You can have my bed, I'll be passed out on the floor somewhere," Tripp said.

Roman thought about what Tripp had said; "Everyone thinks you're cool." It was the secret approval, the moment of acceptance that everyone desired, the confirmation. He felt an intense relief and excitement at the same time. He could hear, in his mind, Tripp saying, "Yeah, that's Roman. He's cool, man, you'll like him." Roman beamed with success. His anxiety, near panic levels already, drifted lightly away for the moment with the flicked ashes of his cigarette. He took another swallow of beer.

"So, where's Betty?" Roman quizzed him sardonically.

"Betty who?"

They laughed. "Not so free-spirited, and careless, huh? Don't even try it. I know you're going to be staying with Betty anyway."

Tripped smiled and changed the subject casually.

"I bet there is a fight. There's always a big brawl. There was one between Scott and Liberty years ago," Tripp said.

"I thought Scott people and Liberty people got along now?"

"There'll be other schools down there, too. Things are a lot different than they were back then."

Roman thought about this fact. He had never really thought about any of the other schools besides Liberty. They were phantoms, outsiders. Scott was mentioned most, always with subtle reverence and resentment. He wanted to meet Scott people—and he wanted to hate them.

"I gotta fucking piss. I've been holding it for half an hour," Tripp said.

They stopped at a bright green gas station just off the road and Tripp went in. Normal, ordinary people getting gas stared at him as he sat in the car. Being high gave everything a strangeness, a flippant dismissal of reality. Tripp came out with another six-pack and a couple of packs of Camel Lights. His fake ID had worked. They pulled out of the station and again were on their way. Roman could feel the high wearing off and asked about another joint. He lit it and as he smoked was calmer than before, was finally what he thought of as mellow.

"In Seaside, we have what's called 'Beach Week,' but since we lived at the beach it wasn't really a big deal," Roman said finally, feeling talkative.

"A week!" Tripp cried, "I'd come home in a body bag. That sounds fucking awesome. Here you just get three nights, two, really. It's all chance. If you're not in the right place at the right time, you could miss something big. Last year, I came down on a Thursday after school. It got ugly fast. Anyway, we partied all night and I drove back to school on one hour of sleep. Had to. If I didn't go to that class that morning I would have failed for the year. Anyway, I fell asleep in that class. The teacher woke me up and told me I smelled like hell and that I should probably leave before I got in trouble. I don't remember a lot from that night."

"I wouldn't think so."

Roman was flipping through the radio stations again.

"Stop there!" Tripp shouted. "Go back!"

"What is it?"

"The Doors. Man, I love this shit." Tripp started singing along. "This shit really makes me feel like getting fucked up."

Roman had heard of The Doors. He thought for a minute about what Tripp said and smiled.

Jim Morrison's deep baritone belted out lyrics with a raspy sneer: "The day destroys the night. Night divides the day."

After about half an hour Roman noticed the faint rippled blueness of water on the horizon to his right. As more of the sound came into view, he could look across and see a strip of land, populated with the colored squares of beach houses, boats on the water, and large hotels rising into the sky.

"This is it," Tripp said as they rounded a curve and started their way up the bridge over to the barrier islands. From the top, Roman could better see how thin and fragile the island was. Stilted houses neatly abutted sandy beaches and the undrinkable, endless ocean beyond it. Tripp finished his sixth beer at the top of the bridge, crushed the can, and flung it into the back seat.

After the bridge Tripp stopped at a wide intersection. Traffic was heavy; windows were down, music was blasting, people were walking briskly on sidewalks, smiling, basking in the sunlight. Roman was deep in his thoughts, taking in the scenery as they rode in silence for a while. Tripp was alert and focused, on a mission. As they drove slowly down the streets, they smoked another joint, hiding it as cars passed.

They drove around, stopping to ask questions of people walking, biking, seemingly lost, trying to get directions to addresses Tripp had scribbled on a piece of paper, even stopping at public phones to make calls. Tripp was trying to find Frank. Finally, they made their way down a small sliver of dirt road, almost indiscernible, to a small trailer. Outside there were guys standing around, laughing and drinking; Roman could tell they were already drunk. They greeted Tripp, who knew them, and Roman was introduced.

"You guys got any weed?" Tripp asked.

"Yeah," one of the guys said, "go inside."

Inside there was a drinking game going on at the coffee table, people Roman had seen at school but did not know. They all looked somehow changed, unlike their school selves, as if his impressions were all wrong, as if a secret was exposed. All eyes turned to the newcomers. The girls, in unison, screamed "Tripp!" and they got up, careful with their beers, and hugged him. Tripp introduced Roman. A pipe was immediately handed to Tripp. He took a hit of it and handed it off to Roman.

"You guys grab a beer," the girls all said.

Tripp and Roman both went in the small kitchen to the fridge, which was packed full of beer. They pulled two cans of Budweiser out, popped the tops, and gulped them. One of the guys in the game got up and came over to them. "Frank!" Tripp said, shaking his hand.

"We've been looking all over for you," Tripp said, almost exasperated.

"What do you think of the trailer?" Frank asked.

"It's cool as shit," Tripp said. Roman agreed, nodding.

"It's my uncle's. He's letting me use it this weekend."

"Where's the weed? You got anything for sale?" Tripp leaned into Frank and whispered.

"Follow me," he said with a wink.

They stumbled through the living room drinking game and went down a narrow hall to a back room. In the room were four guys Roman had never seen, engrossed in conversation. They all stopped when the new arrivals came in the room. Roman felt awkward but when Frank asked one of the guys if he had a quarter for sale, they all seemed to relax.

"You want kind bud or commercial?" the only shirtless guy—who, to Roman, seemed to be the ringleader—asked. He looked a little older than a high schooler.

"Kind," Tripp said.

"Nice," he said, half grinning, half clenching a cigarette in his mouth. He opened a drawer and pulled out a rolled plastic bag and handed it to Tripp. Tripp inspected it, opening it up and smelling it. Roman looked on. All action in the room had stopped and was focused on the transaction. Tripp took a $100 bill and a twenty out of his pocket and gave it to Frank, who handed it to the guy. The room relaxed, conversation resumed, and Roman noticed there was a mirror on the bureau from which the bag had been taken, and a small mountain of white powder sat on it. One of the guys talking went over to the mirror, still talking, with a short straw, and with a razor blade cut two lines. He leaned over the mirror and snorted a line, then held his head back, grabbed his nose, and sniffed loudly. He looked at Roman and held out the straw.

"You want any?"

Roman had never seen cocaine before and was only vaguely aware of its existence—he had heard of its use among the most nefarious characters. But he was still feeling drunk and in an agreeable mood. Looking at the powder, and not wanting to offend the guy, he took the straw, almost automatically, fumbled with it a bit, and did his best to snort. He immediately felt a surge. His head went numb, and his nasal passages opened up. Euphoric, he blinked rapidly and took a deep breath. The drug's intensity became all too real. He desperately needed something to calm himself as two people were talking to him simultaneously and, when he looked down and realized he was holding a beer, felt relief as he raised it and poured the rest of it straight down his throat and asked if he could have another.

"Sure," Frank said. "Mi casa es su casa."

Roman made his back down the hall, stepping carefully through the drinking game group, and was back in the kitchen. He took another beer from the fridge. A girl sitting on the floor glanced at him and he nodded. One girl, raven-haired, pretty, in an orange bikini top and short jeans shorts, was smiling at him. He watched the game and saw a pipe being passed around. There was screaming and laughing in the haze of afternoon light, a fog of smoke, and Roman wanted to say something, wanted to join in, but remained silent and cautious. When he saw Tripp appear out of the back room, he was relieved. The girl, passing by him and getting a beer from the fridge, stopped, and addressed Roman with a flirty smile. "I'm Jill. Do you want to play?"

"Sure," Roman uttered, barely, out of his numb mouth—but no one noticed. He gulped half his beer on the move as Jill took his hand and led him over to the game. "Sit here," she ordered, without looking at him, in a childlike whisper, her voice still an abstraction, as she sat down and patted the spot beside her.

Roman sat down. "What's the game?" he asked and looked around at the players, who all now seemed to be scrutinizing him.

"High or Low. It's easy, you just guess whether the next card is higher or lower. If you're wrong, you have to drink. If you're right a bunch of times you can give those drinks away and make anyone you want drink," she explained. "It's the best game in the world."

More room was made for Tripp, who sat down beside Roman on the floor, and the game resumed. A couple of hours passed, the room becoming livelier, as more people arrived and filled every inch of it. The stereo, playing a mix of classic rock and alternative grunge, pulsed through the small trailer, just above conversation level. The guys in the back came out after a while and resumed their conversation in the kitchen. Cards were slammed, laughter rang out, orders to drink were shouted, and a warm sense of drunkenness came over Roman. He was giddy and happy. More weed was smoked. Roman met and learned everyone's name and the day passed. They went outside, the sun hot, the sky cloudless, and sat on the tailgate of a truck, straddled coolers, and in sat in beach chairs as people arrived urgently and left breathlessly. Late in the afternoon they realized they hadn't been to the beach. Everyone gathered themselves and marched down the street in the dying afternoon light to the wooden steps that gave beach access, their thumping footfalls shaking the staircase. The tide was out, and they stepped on hot sand. Those without shoes sprinted down to the water. Roman dove into the ocean; the cold water woke him up and he felt better. Jill was next to him, smiling at him in a way he knew meant she liked him. They were close in the water and Roman wanted madly to kiss her. He took her hand in the water and pulled her close to him. He embraced her, the water up to their necks, the waves, as they rolled in, floating them up and down, his hands feeling the softness of her back and her arms around him, and her breathing, her life so close to his, and it made him feel bold. He closed his eyes. Her lips were soft, and salty. A splash of water came at them.

"That's fucking gross," Tripp groaned, splashing them again, as more swimmers surrounded them. They separated and laughed at themselves. They went up on the beach and dried off, lounging in the sand, in the cool afternoon sun. Tripp, Roman, and Jill led a group back to the trailer, while others lingered on the beach. A bottle of whiskey appeared, and they passed it around. The kitchen emptied and was darker now; Roman put out a cigarette in an empty beer can and Tripp was beside him. Jill had disappeared.

Tripp leaned over to him. "Let's go to Augustus's house," he said.

Tripp could see Roman about to go look for Jill and grabbed his arm.

"There'll be more there," Tripp said.

Roman and Tripp went out to the car and drove away from the trailer. They said nothing for a time, the day still buzzing in their heads. It was dark, the air was cool, the headlights of cars sped by, and the neon signs were lit. At a large intersection Tripp saw some guys he knew and called over to them.

"Where you guys going?" he asked.

"Augustus's," they said.

"We'll follow you," Tripp shouted.

It was after dark when the two finally found the house they were looking for. It was a gaudy yellow, stucco-sided mansion of immense proportions, with a lookout tower and a veranda on the roof, surrounded by grassy dunes. Roman glimpsed the faint movement of people up on the veranda and heard calls from above. He waved to them automatically. Floodlights illuminated the vast lawn, the grass clipped short. Every window was lit and Roman could see people inside, moving, standing, and the entire spectacle was like a lighthouse beacon, an invitation to celebration. The house was three stories high with balconies and decks wrapping around the first two floors.

They went to the door and were let in by a cute little blonde who didn't look old enough to be there. Roman and Tripp followed her and with a wave she said, "This is it," and vanished into the crowd. In the first room they came to, they were met by some guys Tripp knew and he introduced Roman.

"You guys want to get high?" Tripp asked.

They went up the stairs and into a room people were leaving to rejoin the party. Roman sat on a bed. The unknown guy who sat next to Tripp informed them that they were already fucked up. Tripp said, "We are too." Roman smoked and, in the quiet of the room, could hear the inexhaustible bass thump of music playing downstairs. He talked to several of the guys and girls who came in and they asked where he was from. Beer after beer was brought in and Roman again lost track of time.

The room, cool and breezy, gave him a chill and he got up, told Tripp he was going to look around, and went downstairs. He realized a few hours had passed and there were a great many more people in the house. He pushed his way through the crowd, sidetracked by several drunk people high fiving him and starting conversations on his way to the kitchen. He got out a beer and found himself talking to another girl who was fascinated with the glass she had found in the kitchen and was drinking out of. He could hear chanting out on the deck through an open window and wanted to check it out, but the girl's friend had arrived, and they now had him cornered. The girls suggested joining a game of quarters that was going on at the kitchen table next to them. As the quarters bounced off the marble kitchen table and there was the clink of made shots, Roman felt himself sliding past the point of drunkenness—he was moving into delirium. The room started to pulse and he felt dizzy. A ceiling fan whirred overhead. He decided he needed some fresh air and excused himself, stumbling away from the game and leaning against a wall and heard music. He headed toward it. He found it hard to stand up straight and it took more effort to think and get the words out of his throat. There, in the heart of the gaiety, he saw an interesting figure, Adonis-like, substantially built, lounging on a pulled-out sleeper sofa, shirtless and shoeless, in red swim trunks and, on either side of him, a tremendously pretty girl leaning in close to him, apparently whispering into his ear. He had a beer bottle in one hand and a cigarette in the other.

Roman watched this scene with a vague curiosity. "Who is that?" Roman asked a passerby. "That's Augustus," the stranger said incredulously and walked off. Roman had heard the name but had never seen him. Augustus, from what he had heard, bordered on the mythical to these people. Roman had never heard anything bad said about him, which was strange for someone who was so obviously envied.

One song ended and another began. There were shouts and clamoring from the deck. Roman moved on, looking around for someone he knew, but saw nothing but unfamiliar faces. He staggered through the sea of bodies, trying to find the bathroom. Once located, he looked at a long line of waiting faces staring at him. He squeezed back through the living room as the lights suddenly went off, and people roared. Through blaring music and dancing bodies, he went out onto the deck. There were people packed tightly and tranquil chatter, soothing in the moonlight. Roman felt better in the night air. He looked out and saw that the party did not stop at the deck. There was a vast sea of heads stretching out into the sand dunes and on toward the sound of crashing waves. The night sky was overhead and the comet hung still in its nightly place.

Roman wished some of his friends back in Seaside could see this party. Here in this citadel, on the watery edge of oblivion, was God—and great sacrifices were being made. Roman made his way down the zigzagged walkway to the beach and he stepped with relief into the sand. People turned and eyed him only briefly and went back to their conversations. He could see the silver shine of beer cans in every hand and tripped over a cooler. Saving his beer with a graceful twist, he walked along the dunescape looking for a place sufficiently dark to take a piss. Instead, he threw up. After the heaving was over, he felt better. He stumbled through the dunes and found another place to relieve himself. Admiring the blowing grasses of the dunes and glint of the stars in the sky, he heard the engine of a four-wheeled ATV approaching. He turned as he pissed, unnoticed, and saw that the police had snuck up on the party by way of the beach. He hurried back up the deck to find Tripp, who was inside the house sitting on the side of Augustus's palatial bed. He whispered in Tripp's ear.

"The cops are here."

"Where?"

"The beach."

"Shit!"

Tripp turned to tell Augustus, who seemed indifferent. "Dude. This is your place. You got to get out of here."

Augustus, suddenly grasping his predicament even through his haze and nonchalance, rose, leaving the girls. The three guys decided the beach was the best path of escape. They jumped over the wooden railing of the deck and landed in the soft, grassy sand of the dunes. Roman peered around a dune and saw the police were occupied. He waved Tripp and Augustus toward him. The crowd was vacating the beach in droves. The three of them slipped along the dunes until the lights and noise of the house were gone. They climbed a dune, Roman stopping at the top to look back one last time at the blazing house, then he went down and sat with Tripp and Augustus in a valley to decide their next move.

"Oh, fuckin' shit, man! They're gonna to be passing out a shitload of tickets," Tripp said, giggling to himself. "It's a good thing you got out of there, Augustus."

Augustus only scoffed slightly and pulled out a pint of whiskey he had stashed in his back pocket on the way out. He unsteadily unscrewed the cap.

"Well, the night's not a total loss," he said, slurring, then taking a swig from the bottle. Roman wondered, as drunk as he was, how he could even still drink. Augustus handed the bottle over automatically to Roman, who took it and drank from it. Roman could feel his heart beating fast, his buzz disappearing.

"Easy, dude," Augustus said and, taking the bottle back, took another large gulp.

"What the fuck do we do now?" Tripp asked, in a general way, standing up and surveying the scene.

"We should chill for a while. The cops are going to be swarming that place, they're going to be canvassing and shit," Roman said.

"Man, I don't see any cops or anybody. The road has to be just over there," Tripp said, pointing. "Let's go."

They got up and crept unsteadily through the sand dunes, grasses cutting at Roman's ankles. Augustus stumbled and fell into the sand, laughing at himself. Roman pulled him up and helped him walk. The sandy dunes were desolate and reflected the moonlight as the trio trudged up and down them trying to find a way out. Roman could not tell where they were going. He tried to keep the sound of the ocean behind him and Tripp's footfalls ahead of him. The rush of the escape had faded, along with Augustus's ability to walk. Augustus fell again and Roman picked him up, placing one of Augustus's arms over his shoulder as they walked.

"Thanks, dude. Having—hic—a bit of a time walking. And seeing, for that matter," Augustus said.

Tripp was ahead of them when they reached the line of beach cottages. Roman could see Tripp out near the road, looking both ways. He came back to the dune behind a cottage where Roman and Augustus had stopped to sit down.

"You guys wait here, I'll go get the car," Tripp said.

Roman tried to be as quiet as possible. Augustus was slumped against him, the pint still in hand, mumbling inaudibly.

"Where?" Augustus muttered.

Roman turned, took the pint from him, took another gulp, and grimaced. He was no longer feeling a buzz and desperately wanted it back. He pulled out a cigarette and handed it to Augustus, lighting it for him.

"Hey. That's mine," Augustus said grabbing the bottle back. "I'm just kiddin'. You can have some," he said, sheepish and childlike. Roman took the bottle back and put the cap on it.

"Hey... where are we?" Augustus uttered, looking straight up into the stars. His head jerked forward, and Augustus shut one eye and looked at Roman.

"Do I know you?" Augustus asked. Roman said nothing.

"Whoever you are, I can see four of you," he said, holding up his hand and showing four fingers.

"Yeah, man. I'll bet you can."

"You don't have to be mean," Augustus said, and flopped on his back down in the sand.

Roman saw headlights coming toward them and prayed that it wasn't cops. The car stopped and Tripp stuck his head out with a smile. "Get in, you fuckheads." Roman helped Augustus up and put him in the back seat, then went around and got in the front, kicking empty beer cans out of the way.

"What's going on back at the house?" Roman asked. Tripp looked happy, like a man who had just gotten away with something.

"Everybody up there is busted, man. I think we're the only ones who got out," Tripp said with a gleeful giggle.

"Who's busted?" Augustus blurted out to no one.

"So, where the fuck are we supposed to stay now?" Roman asked.

"Easy, man. There are a lot of places."

"Have you ever seen so many hot girls?" Augustus said. "Who were those girls?"

"You used to date those girls."

"Really?" Augustus asked mirthfully. Tripp turned the car at a stop sign. Roman lit another cigarette and watched the stilted cottages pass by while Tripp found a radio station. On the main strip Roman felt relieved they had avoided drinking tickets. Roman and Tripp said little as the car moved swiftly down the narrow beach roads.

"Hey, I know you," Augustus said from the back seat, leaning forward in the space between Tripp and Roman's seats. "You're the new guy."

Roman said nothing and flicked some ash from his cigarette out the window.

"See, I can tell you're cool. You don't know me from shit and could fucking care less and I dig that shit," Augustus said. Roman could smell the acrid aroma of liquor, beer, and cigarettes on Augustus's breath and tried to look out the window.

"I like you, dude. So, I'm going to tell you. No. I'm going to ask you. Have you ever been in love? I was so in love with this girl. Not those fucking girls back at the party, but my point is I was in love.

And you know what? It wasn't enough. This girl was awesome, man. Beautiful. Smart. But different, man. Be careful, dude. Of those girls that want to change you. Now I'm some reject. Like Frankenstein's monster."

"More like Jekyll and Hyde," Tripp said smugly.

"Don't listen to him," Augustus said, "He's jealous cause I get all the girls. And that's what you got to do, new guy. All the girls love the new guy. You gotta use that."

"Sit back, drunk ass," Tripp ordered.

Augustus flopped back into the back seat and Roman could hear him push empty beer cans out of the seat beside him. Roman looked back to see Augustus lying down.

"Hey, new guy?"

"Yeah?" Roman answered.

"What's your name?"

Roman was about to answer when he heard Augustus snoring in the back seat.

"Oh, shit" Tripp said.

Roman saw a blue flash. Fuck. Cops. Tripp pulled the car over to the side of the road. Roman looked at Tripp, who shook his head.

"We're fucked," was all Tripp said, as he pounded the steering wheel.

"Relax, man. You're sober," Roman said.

The officer walked up to the car, shining his light in the windows. Tripp rolled down his window.

"What's up, guys?" the officer asked. Roman thought this greeting was strange. "Looks like you boys have had a bit to drink tonight," he said.

"No, sir" Tripp said. Roman felt the pint in his pocket.

"Then who drank all of these?" he indicated with the flashlight, pointing at the empty beer cans littering Tripp's car.

"He did," Tripp said, pointing his thumb toward the back seat at Augustus. "We were just trying to get him home. It's his car."

"And you haven't had anything to drink?" he asked. Roman searched his mind for how many beers Tripp had had but could not come up with a number. He looked at his friend but was too drunk himself to tell whether Tripp was.

"No, sir," Tripp said.

"Well. You kids get out of here. Keep it between the ditches," was all he said, and he was gone. The blue flashing lights turned off and the cop sped away from them. Tripp and Roman were in too much shock to move.

"Dude. I think you should drive before he comes back," Roman said.

"Did that just happen?" Tripp asked.

Roman took the pint out and took a gulp as they pulled out. Tripp took one as well. The last thing Roman remembered was blurry. They finished the pint in the car, smoked a cigarette, and then there was a white motel.

Roman woke up in the morning on the floor in a small room with two beds. As he got up, he noticed a mound of sheets on the floor and people in each of the small beds. As quietly as he could, he went out the door and fished around in his pockets for a cigarette. There was one left. His head was pounding. He saw Tripp's car and walked over to it, figuring Augustus would still be in there, asleep. Roman looked through the still-rolled down rear window into the back seat where Augustus had been just hours before, but he was gone, only the scattered beer cans and the empty pint littered the seat. Roman closed the door and kicked the tire, making sure it was all real and not just some phantom summer dream.

SIX

Roman, feeling dizzy, went back into the motel room. A blast of cold air, generated by a large humming window unit, hit his face as he opened the door and he felt, aside from relief, a momentary deathlike light-headedness. The room was frigid like a tomb, full of snoring. He closed the door quietly behind him and tried to ignore the pounding in his head, snare-drumish, and the ache, unholy, between his eyes. Mobility was almost impossible in the small wood-paneled room, and there were two small double beds occupying most of it. One of the beds managed somehow to hold three guys. Dean, sprawled on his back, was on the left, his arm across Edwin's head—Roman thought that was his name—who was on the right, and the third, Ronnie, was curled up in a ball, barely balancing on the edge at the foot of the bed, a towel draped over him, his right arm a pillow. On the other bed were two guys Roman didn't know. He had not slept well on the floor with a stack of towels for a pillow, but he recalled periods of blankness—which was enough—and the sound of the air conditioner in the glimpses of night that passed. He stepped forward, toward the nightstand, to look through the packs of cigarettes for another one to smoke when he stepped on something mushy and organic beneath the mound of white sheets.

"Oww!" he heard a muffled groan.

He had stepped on Tripp, who promptly stuck his head out from under the white pillowy wad, eyes squinty and grimacing.

"What the fuck are you doing up," Tripp said, not really asking.

"Couldn't sleep any longer on this damn floor," Roman said.

Tripp yawned. "Yeah, I know. It fucking sucks." Tripp slowly got up, sheets falling away from him. "What time is it?"

Roman looked over at the clock. "Nine."

"Well, I guess that's long enough," he shrugged on the way to the bathroom. "What time did we go to bed?" Tripp asked from behind the door. Roman heard Tripp rummaging through the ice of a cooler.

"I don't fucking know. The whole night is a blur."

Tripp came out of the bathroom with two beers dripping ice-cold water. Roman took one, the can cold to the touch, popped the top, drank from it, swallowing hard, and thought of the terrible taste in his mouth.

"This will fix you right up," Tripp said, doing the same.

"Whose place is this? Who are these guys?" Roman asked.

"Shut up," one of the sleeping bodies said.

"Fuck you," Tripp answered. "The guy over there snoring is Dean, beside him is Edwin. You know Ronnie. The other two guys are Gary and his buddy. Where's Augustus?" Tripp asked, while lighting a cigarette he pulled from a crushed pack in his pocket.

"He's gone."

"Where the fuck did he go?" Roman shrugged and took a huge drag and another awful gulp. Tripp sat down on the bed.

"Would you two shut the fuck up?" Gary said, not opening his eyes.

"We need more beer," Tripp said.

"Go fuck yourself. The hell you do. I've bought you guys over 10 cases this weekend." Gary sat up and rubbed his eyes. "What the fuck are you guys doing here?" he asked.

"We crashed here last night. Don't you remember?"

"Jeezz… this place is full of dudes. Where are those high school chicks? Today is a finding chicks day. Wasn't bad for a high school party," Gary said.

"Were you at Augustus's?" Roman asked.

"Hell, yeah. Where were you?"

"We were there," Tripp said. "Toward the end."

"We left when the cops showed up. They passed out a bunch of tickets. Some guy got arrested."

"Who?"

"Some young fucker. Parents probably had to come get him."

Roman thought about their narrow escape as he took another gulp of his beer. He wanted to throw up, but he forced another gulp down. A few more and he would be back into it, feeling it again, the doomed ride of Junior/Senior.

"Take us to the store. I'll give you a twenty," Tripp said

Gary threw a pillow at Tripp and rose from the bed. "I need cigarettes anyway. Can't sleep the day away at the beach. I'll sleep when I'm dead."

They threw on shirts, put on flip-flops and sandals, went out, wincing in the sunlight, and got into Tripp's Honda, all of them still groggy, smelling of ocean, barely awake. The car whined to life, Tripp put it in gear, lurching forward; they were soon on the deserted streets, ghostlike as the day began. The sky was a divine blue, cloudless, hazily humid, and they were quiet as they sped down the main strip. It was Sunday. Retail shops and businesses were dark and shuttered and parking lots were empty except for the McDonald's they passed, which was lively with patrons and a line around the building for the drive-thru. Roman looked at it and felt the pangs of hunger. They saw a BP and Tripp pulled the Honda in. Tripp handed Gary money from a canvas Velcro wallet. Gary took the money, hopped out of the car, and went inside. Tripp and Roman, sitting in the car, kept a vigilant lookout and tried to look older. Gary came out—the sight of him satisfying—with two cases of Budweiser he put it in the back seat next to Roman. Roman reached over and put his hand on the cases and a chill went through him.

Back at the motel Roman first saw the sign for where they had spent the night. The painted white wooden sign read "The Beach Inn" and one of the "n's" was missing. Underneath, in smaller letters, hung on a hook, were the words "No Vacancy." After parking, Tripp and Roman put the beer in the trunk cooler and slammed the lid down. Gary was looking at them, smoking in front of the motel, and shaking his head. Ronnie came out the door behind him, hair askew, in boxers, squinting in the light, and stretched his arms out and yawned.

"What's up?" he said. Gary just looked at him and turned back to Roman and Tripp.

"You guys look like Christmas morning," Gary said. "Remember. Anybody asks? You found that beer."

"Thanks, Gary," Roman and Tripp said at the same time, and they got in the car and sped away.

"Where to?" Tripp asked.

"Let's run through the circle first and check out the waves, then go by Augustus's house."

They cruised down the sunny morning streets, feeling the worn languor of the city. They drove with the windows down and the music off. The city was lazy and the shabby stilted houses kept their still, sleepy, calm as the guys arrived at the circle. The circle park had a city block to itself and there was a miniature golf course beside a deserted amusement park with its monstrous, motionless Ferris wheel, its vacant gondolas swinging slightly in the breeze, and a towering bungee-jumping platform soaring into the emptiness overhead, its bumper cars parked in a line, ready for the day's guests. The circle was one-way traffic and they parked in a diagonal space. They walked past painted building walls and an open arcade, the machines on and making beeps and tones but unused, and then across a parking lot where moms, dads, children, and grandparents were getting beach chairs and coolers out of SUVs and minivans for a day at the beach. Gulls cackled overhead, circling like the scavengers they are, begging in a high-pitched chorus of shrill vocalizations. Roman and Tripp crossed the wooden boardwalk and walked out to where the sand began. People were already set up, dotting the beach with colorful parasols. Crabs scattered out of the way. Roman stopped, eyes keen and focused, and surveyed the surf, sliding up the dark sand. The tide was in and there were surfers sitting on boards, bobbing in the waves. One, seeing something promising, turned and started paddling, caught a wave, stood up and cut left for a short ride, then fell over on his side and disappeared beneath the foamy water. Roman felt a different ache, a yearning. He hadn't surfed since last summer. He thought about his forgotten board in the shed.

"Some pretty good waves out there," Tripp said. "You surf, don't you?"

"Yeah," Roman said, "a little bit."

They went back to the car and drove off. Down the main strip again and, after making several zigzagging turns, they came to the house from the night before. Roman thought the house looked even more pompous in the daylight. Roman and Tripp parked beside the road and walked along the long brick driveway and up the steps. There were various abandoned cars scattered across the lawn. The door was open, so they went in. The house was different in the daylight, less the center of decadence and more a family's possession. The house was trashed; a wasteland of silver beer cans lined the room and there was the odor of stale beer and cigarettes. The stereo was still on, but the volume was turned down and the TV was in the same state. There were surfboards Roman had not noticed the night before against the wall. The decor of the house was like that of the Beach Inn, bright yellow furniture and beachscape prints on the walls, the trinkets of shells, nets, and carved wooden fish. Roman wondered what Augustus's parents would think if they saw the place this way. Augustus, the only mortal visible, still in his red bathing suit, was sleeping in a mess of sheets on the sleeper sofa that had been his throne the night before. The girls were long gone and, where Roman had felt envy of him the night before, the stark reality of the almost-abandoned house evoked a brief wave of sympathy. There was a fast-food bag on the kitchen table and Tripp looked in it.

Smiling, he pulled out two biscuits and tossed one to Roman. They sat on barstools at the counter and devoured the meal as a breeze blew through the two open sliding glass doors to the deck. Roman could hear the chirping of insects and the hollow, unrelenting sound of crashing surf. The air conditioning was off and flies landing, then buzzing around.

"Should we wake him?" Tripp asked.

"Let him sleep," Roman advised, and got up and closed the sliding glass doors.

"This place is a disaster. Glad I don't have to clean this up. We should get out of here before he wakes up," Tripp said.

Tripp rummaged through the kitchen. Roman went upstairs investigating, looking for survivors. He looked in the bedrooms for signs of life. Everyone must have split, he thought. Every room had the pallid grimness of a just-abandoned space. One door was closed. He opened it slightly and inside, on the bed, were a couple, asleep. He looked at them for a minute. Finding nothing of interest, he went back downstairs and out onto the deck. The large deck looked emptier than it should have; chairs were scattered about and the table was so full that not one more beer can could be squeezed on to it. On the railing, a line of beer cans went from one end of the deck to the other. It had an ordered, artsy look, Roman had to admit. Improvised ashtrays, beer bottles, kitchen glasses, and plates, were everywhere, with half-smoked butts piled high and overflowing. Roman saw the beer funnel over the rail, down in the dunes. He climbed down to retrieve the night's favorite relic. It had been a good party; the night had had an energy to it that was now gone, the house was used up. It had been the place to be—and that was all—he could honestly not remember having ever been to a party like it.

"Hell of a party, wasn't it?" Tripp came out on the deck.

"Yeah."

"It's all they'll be talking about for a while."

It was all anyone really needed, Roman thought, some new thing to talk about. Something they had gotten away with. Tripp was over by the keg pumping. He squeezed the tap. Nothing. He shrugged his shoulders.

"What the hell. It was worth a shot."

Tripp went back to the kitchen, made a space, and started rolling a joint on the counter. Roman, for some reason, washed out the funnel. Tripp went over to one of the couches and sat down. Roman sat next to him. They passed the joint back and forth, inhaling and blowing out thick clouds of smoke. Exhaling, Roman could feel the thick smoke leaving his lungs. The TV, on some random channel, suddenly became very important to him and he wondered if he should turn it off. Roman got up and did so, feeling relieved. Tripp, perplexed but saying nothing, took a big hit off the joint and was overcome by a violent, spastic cough.

"If you don't cough, you don't get off," he said finally, his eyes watery.

When Roman was stoned, he sometimes could not tell if he was enjoying it or not, as he felt the imagined wavelengths in his mind trailing off into an infinite absence. He tried to focus on the calm beach sounds of wind, insects, and waves. Tomorrow he would be back in his unrecognizable new world, but he would know a little more about it. A dread overcame him that made him think again about more immediate concerns, like where they were going to stay that night. He thought of the police returning to the scene of the crime and finding them there, stoned, with a bag of weed. He felt a strong urge to just leave Tripp there, walk to a pay phone, and call his father to come get him, to avert certain disaster. Instead, he asked Tripp where they should go next. Somewhere, anywhere but there, Roman thought.

"Gimme a minute. I'm too fucked up to drive."

Tripp handed Roman what was left of the joint. Roman put it in an ashtray next to the slumbering Augustus. Tripped coughed and lit a cigarette.

"What a fucking party, man."

Roman nodded and began to feel at ease once more.

They hung around the house for an hour, hoping someone would stop by. They walked out onto the beach to check the waves. On the beach, Tripp saw three guys he knew, in beach chairs with a cooler beside them, drinking beers.

"What's up?" Tripp asked.

"Just chillin'," said the guy closest to him. "You want a beer?"

"Sure," Tripp said, and two were dug out of the cooler. One was tossed to Roman, who opened it slowly.

"Roman, this is Jimmy, Will, and Hunter." They all shook hands. "So, what happened last night? Tripp asked.

"Dude, it was fucked up. I'm standing there talking to this really hot Liberty girl when I turn around and a cop is standing right there. He's just looking at me. He asks me if I'm drinking and I'm standing there with a beer in my hand, so I say 'Ah, no, someone just handed this to me.' What the fuck was I supposed to say? Anyway, he didn't buy it—surprise—and he takes me out to the police car for a drinking ticket. Long story short, I go back up to the house to find the girl and she was gone."

"Damn, dude. That sucks," Tripp said. They all agreed.

"You're damn right it sucks. Finger of God. What happened to you guys?"

"Roman saw the cops outside and came and got me. I got Augustus and we split into the dunes. We were so drunk we didn't know where we were."

"You guys were lucky. All three of us got tickets. They gave out over 50 drinking tickets. I think they got one guy for possession and arrested him."

Roman listened while watching the waves and the people coming over the beach accesses and setting up their stuff for the day.

"Is Augustus still asleep?"

"Yeah," Tripp said. At the mention of Augustus, Roman's attention returned.

"That dude was out of control last night," Jimmy said, "I saw him funnel about twenty beers. One time he did three beers."

The guy in the middle chair spoke up. "Dude was on a mission."

"Did you hear about him trying to talk to that girl?"

They all shook their heads no.

"All right, well, it's Natalie, you know, church girl, totally out of her element, very rich, really stuck-up, only dates college guys. Who the hell knows why she's there? I mean, hell must have frozen over. Well, Augustus has been after her for years. She broke up with her boyfriend—I found out, so I went and told Augustus. He's a fucking mess but he perks up and says to me, 'Is that right?' and starts to walk in her direction. I tried to stop him. Anyway, apparently, I heard this from one of her friends, but he walks up to her and jumps up on the deck railing beside her and introduces himself and says, get this, 'Forlines, Augustus Forlines,' like he's James Bond or something. Then he falls backward off the deck into the sand dunes."

Laughter erupted among them.

"Natalie is laughing at him and he's down in the dunes, on his back, calling up for help, wanting someone to throw him a rope. A ladder, for Christ's sake. It was the funniest shit I've ever heard."

Roman laughed with a flicker of pity and he wondered just what it was that was haunting Augustus. And why he found himself wondering this he couldn't say.

"Man, that dude is nuts," they all agreed.

"What about the cops?" Tripp asked.

"I don't know where that fool got to, but they were asking whose place it was all night and no one would tell. Everyone just said they had just come and didn't know who the owner was. The cops cleared the house out and left. A couple of us walked down the road to someone else's house, hung out for a while, and then came back to crash."

After chatting about some of the night's other adventures, Roman and Tripp went back up to the house and went inside. Augustus opened his eyes briefly, rolled over on the bed, and went back to snoring. For a minute, Roman thought he might wake up. He wished Augustus would wake up so he could meet him, but he didn't, so they left him there in that big house to his hangover, his haunting, and his disaster.

"Where to next?" Roman asked.

"Got to go over to Patricia's and face the music."

"Who's over there?" Roman asked.

"It's where the senior girls are staying."

They got into Tripp's Honda and sped in the morning sunlight down the narrow beach streets. Roman, reminded of beach days back home, felt the slight sunburn beneath his shirt. He was finally feeling at peace with his surroundings, was swept with a sense of clarity. His high wearing off, the beach and day looked more brilliant, a whiff of drying seaweed filled his nose, and he was filled with a sense of hope and a feeling that anything could happen.

Nora was putting her bathing suit on and looking at herself in the mirror. She turned side to side, stopping and posing. Feeling self-conscious, she put her hair in a ponytail and began packing a bag for the beach. What else, she wondered, holding her chin and tapping her lips with one finger. Fuck it, she thought to herself, put her sunglasses on, and went out of the room.

"What's up, girl?" Patricia said from the kitchen.

Patricia was standing in the kitchen eating cereal. Beside her was her boyfriend Martin trying, with a spoon, to eat from her bowl. She leaned into him, pushing him away with her shoulder. He tried again and she slapped his hand away with her free hand.

"You guys ready yet?" Nora asked.

"Waiting on you hos," Martin said.

"Very classy," Nora mumbled.

"Betty's still not back from the store. Everyone else is on the porch and ready," Patricia said through a mouthful of cereal.

The room was bathed in sunlight, the windows open, the day's sparkling freshness just glinting through the glass. Nora, glad to be out of the small, dark room that was hers, walked past them and out through the screen door to the second-floor porch and sat in one of the white rocking chairs with Linda and Kim, who were engrossed in conversation.

"Hey, girl!" Linda called.

"Hey," she uttered.

Nora, her legs crossed, felt their smoothness with one hand, and looked at her watch, the one Augustus had given her. It was 10:30 AM and she wondered why she was still wearing that watch.

Tripp's Honda pulled into the driveway beneath them. The girls all stopped and stood up to see who the arrivals were. Roman and Tripp got out and came up the stairs.

"What's up, ladies?" Tripp said with his arms outstretched, grinning playfully.

"You guys look like shit," Linda said.

"You're in big fucking trouble, man," Nora said gravely.

"What did I do?" Tripp shrugged.

"You know what."

"I guess I better go in there and face the music."

"I don't know. She's pretty pissed. I think she's done with you," Nora said.

Tripp looked worried and hurried up the stairs, leaving Roman standing there, awkwardly, not really knowing anyone. Roman sat down quietly in one of the rocking chairs.

"Hey," Linda asked Roman, "where'd you guys stay last night?"

"You don't even want to know," he said.

The girls were all amused by this.

"We ended up in some roach motel. Seven of us in a room the size of a bathroom."

"You guys go to the party?" Linda asked.

"Yes."

"Good party?"

"Yeah, it was all right."

"We heard it was a rager."

Roman nodded. "It was."

Patricia, followed by Betty, came out of the door in a hurry. "Let's go, girls," she said.

Tripp came out behind Betty, pleading, "Wait a minute can we talk? I'm sorry. Okay. As God as my witness, Roman made me go to that party instead of stopping by here first. Didn't you, Roman?"

They all turned and looked at Roman. Nora's eyebrows went up in a sarcastic "Hmm." He looked back at her, froze for a minute, and shrugged.

"Yeah, I made him go," Roman nodded.

Nora laughed. "Yeah, right."

Tripp got ahold of Betty and pulled her close. "Last night was guy's night. Remember? I'm yours all day." Everyone groaned.

"You're making us sick," Nora said. "Forgive him and let's get on with it."

"You have to carry our stuff," Betty said. Tripp started to say something, but Betty gave him a fierce, not to be messed with, look.

"There's the cooler and the volleyball set," Patricia said, pointing down at the items.

The girls marched down the stairs while Roman and Tripp picked up the beach gear. Heavily loaded, Roman and Tripp trudged out to the beach behind the girls. They put the stuff down at a spot the girls agreed on.

"I'm going back for the beer in the trunk," Tripp said to Roman.

For the first time Nora took notice of Roman, whom she had heard of but had yet to meet.

"A little early, isn't it, dude?" Nora emphasized the last word.

"Never too early, dude," Tripp said back to her, emphasizing the "dude."

The day was bleached in sunlight. The girls put down their towels, sprayed themselves with tanning oil, and laid themselves out. Tripp put his beach chair next to Betty's, who was on the end, and Roman sat on the cooler. Nora went straight for the surf and swam. When she came out, she dried off and turned on the radio. Roman tried not to obviously watch her while Tripp and Betty babbled, without shame, in a playful way. Nora was beautiful, as he had heard. He assumed she had a boyfriend. He knew girls sometimes behaved a certain way when they were in love, it was a sort of playful yet standoffishness. Patricia was single. She hadn't spoken to him at all, even though they had traded glances. A sure sign, he thought, of her interest.

Roman watched the waves for a while and drank beer from a plastic cup. Nothing really worth surfing was out there. He listened for a while to his companions, not really understanding what they were talking about, and felt his skin burning. He put on sunblock out of boredom. He glanced down at the other end of the row, to where Nora was. She was sitting up on her elbows looking off into the water. All of the girls were attractive; Patricia, slight and slender. There was a confident and unapproachable quality to Nora. He found himself comparing his chances between Nora and Patricia, going over scenarios in his head as the day went on. Patricia came over and asked him for a beer. He got her one and poured it in a cup. She gave a half smile and went back to sit down on her towel. More girls arrived, more beer was drunk, and he knew he was in the right place. He was introduced to people he had seen at Liberty but had never spoken to. He talked to Patricia again, beer making her chattier, but he kept looking to Nora to see if she was looking back. But she never was. Cops were spotted on ATVs and everyone froze as they passed.

Finally, Patricia asked Roman about Ronnie, Edwin, and Dean.

"Back at the hotel," Tripp said. "I imagine they'll be here soon."

The group decided to go for a swim. The water was still a little cold, so they all hesitantly eased their way into the waves.

"You just gotta run and–" at that moment, Tripp broke into a run toward the surf and jumped headfirst into the water and came up, shivering and cursing. They all swam out past where the small swell was breaking. The chill of the water cleared Roman's head and he felt fresh and composed—comfortable, even. Patricia was asking about the party as Roman tried to float on his back. She splashed him. He splashed her back. They were face-to-face, shredded green seaweed floating around them. Tiny white triangles bounced on the horizon, but it felt as though the two of them were out there with the whole sea to themselves. Betty and Tripp came out, floating on rafts, to swim with them and the moment was broken. Roman swam in and walked back up on the beach, thinking about Cassandra. A sense of guilt nagged him.

Ronnie, Dean, and Gary arrived, waving and smiling, their bare feet kicking up sand. They set up chairs with the rest of the burgeoning beach colony. Nora, wearing sunglasses and brushing her blonde hair behind her ear, was talking to Dean when Roman came up. Roman wondered when he would get his chance to finally have a conversation with her. He sat down and waited for the right moment. A volleyball net was set up and a game was started. Roman cracked a beer and joined the game because Nora had. She wasted no time and spiked the ball violently, right at him. It bounced off his head and she giggled. The sun was hot and they were all breathless and the game soon dissipated.

Ronnie and Dean wanted to walk and check out some girls on the beach, so Roman went with them. They walked barefoot along the wet sand, the waves sliding up their ankles. Ronnie and Dean saw some girls they knew and went to talk to them; they wanted to hang around for a minute, so Roman walked back alone. He realized he was alone for the first time, anonymous, unknown, and he enjoyed the break. He stopped to pick a broken shell out of the sand. He put it in his pocket and, in the distance, could see the group's set up. As he approached, he looked for Nora, but she was gone. He sat in an empty beach chair next to Patricia.

"Where have you been?"

"Strolling the beach."

"Pick up any chicks?"

"Saw a few."

She reached over and patted his arm. "Maybe next time."

As the day faded, the senior girls and what was left of the guys packed up the beach gear and headed back to the house. Roman and the rest continued to drink beer on the upstairs porch. The commotion of dinner began; they grilled steaks while reggae music played. A game of High or Low began on the deck and lasted into the night. Patricia never left his side for long and he was having a good time with her. When everyone else went inside, they remained on the deck in rocking chairs next to each other and talked for a good while until she excused herself and went inside. He thought she was nice and was thinking about maybe asking her out. Inside the house he could hear indistinct voices. It was the last night. He lit a cigarette. He was enjoying the relative quiet of the evening compared with the night before. He was alone with his thoughts when he heard the screen door creak open. He looked over and it was Nora. She walked up to him and leaned forward on the railing just in front of him, looking out at the dunes and, beyond them, the ocean.

"She's not your type," Nora said, without looking at him.

"Why do you say that?" Roman asked.

"Because you're a nice guy," she said, turning and looking at him for a moment.

"What makes you say that?"

"I can always tell."

"What if I'm not," Roman said, suddenly remembering Cassandra back in Seaside.

"We'll see," Nora said and turned to leave.

"Hey!" he called to her.

Nora stopped but, before he could say anything else, Patricia came out, startling them both, and Nora winked at him in a sly way and went back inside. Patricia sat down and, when she started talking, he wondered what Nora had meant. Later, Nora went to bed and Roman sat out on the porch for a while with Patricia and the others, but soon she too went to bed and his thoughts wandered again. After everyone else had gone to bed he was still sitting on the porch, looking out at the ocean. The city lights blazed over the beach house's roof as the wind stirred and Roman thought about the darkened, empty beach, the eternal, unceasing surf, and understood, perhaps for the first time, that he was very small and the universe very old.

SEVEN

The sky grew darker and storm clouds moved in overhead as Roman drove home from The Pines. When he dropped Tripp off it was 7 p.m.; Tripp had an hour to make it to Liberty High School by 8 p.m. for graduation. Roman parked in his driveway and went up to the house. He stopped on the porch and turned around as he heard the first drops of rain begin to fall, slowly at first, and then steadily rose to a torrent.

Feeling weary, he sat down on the front porch steps, felt around in his pockets for cigarettes, found none, and watched as the water fell steadily off the edge of the tin roof. The sky was a dull gray. His last day of high school, forever, was finally over and he pondered the future not with a sense of achievement, but a matter-of-fact casualness. He heard thunder crack overhead. Would graduation be rained out? He knew it was on the football field. Would it be postponed? He wished he had attended it now, as he sat there and felt lonely. He went in the house, picked up the phone, and dialed Frank's number. Frank was a junior but hung out mostly with Tripp and a bunch of seniors; he lived in a house near Tripp's in The Pines. A woman's voice answered the phone.

"Can I speak to Frank?" Roman asked.

"I'll go get him," the woman answered politely. Roman heard the phone clunk down on what had to be a table and then he heard the woman yell, "Frank, phone!"

A brisk voice answered. Roman told Frank what he was supposed to do.

"All right," Frank said, "I'll be there in a minute."

Roman hung up the phone, then wandered around the house, waiting. He heard a car go by the house out on the road, went to the window, and looked out. Nothing. He went back out the front door and walked the small walkway over to the garage. His father wasn't there, either. Roman was sitting on the front steps again when Frank pulled up into his driveway. Roman got in the car and showed Frank the way to the abandoned house in the woods that he and Tripp had found by chance one recent day.

They drove up the dirt driveway off the old house, parked in front of it, and got out.

"This is perfect," Frank said.

They drove back into Coxville and then on to Martinsboro. Roman looked out the car window as they passed newly nestled subdivision signs between berms, then older neighborhoods and strip mall parking lots. The lustrous newness of the city fell away and the car entered the downtown area with its loaf-like brick businesses abutting one another. All were crammed together, their facades sphinxlike, advertisements everywhere, grainy sidewalks leading to swinging glass doors. They passed the courthouse, its columns rising up, its clock an omniscient eye. Opposite the courthouse sat the Town Commons, a rolling green lawn crossed with sidewalks, dogs being walked, and joggers, which gently slopped down to the Shale River. The river was now familiar to him. Leaving downtown the landscape changed again and Roman saw the red-tiled roofs of the brick university buildings. Across from the university was the oldest neighborhood in Martinsboro, a labyrinth, a dead-end maze, where students rented the aged homes that the middle class had abandoned decades before. The houses were older, much like the ones in Coxville, and there were many of them. Street after street of quaint houses nestled in elaborate, vivid landscapes, no two alike. It was a sort of jungly ancient city, looking almost, but not quite, like modern ruins. They turned onto one of the streets. Roman, unfamiliar with this part of Martinsboro, was uneasy. The area was thickly wooded with broad oaks and alive with life. There seemed everywhere to be someone walking or out in their small yard. There were old sections back in Seaside that were like this, but the houses were much larger. Roman waved at the college students sitting on porches drinking beer. The neighborhood held secrets and imparted conflicting senses of warning and invitation.

"This is where all the students live," Frank said.

Roman nodded.

"You going to school here next year?" Frank asked.

"I don't know. Where are we going?" Roman responded.

"We're going over to this guy's house we know who buys us beer."

They drove slowly down the street, passing unkempt yards and cars parked on the curbs of the narrow streets and cracked sidewalks broken by roots. The all-round shabbiness of this area gave it a feeling of impermanence, a sense of "just passing through."

The university, he knew, had a notorious reputation as a party school. Roman was intimidated by the way people spoke of it. He had been accepted there but, in his mind, it materialized to Roman as some vortex of debauchery. Yet there was also a quaint atmosphere to the campus and neighborhood. As they moved out of the older section they came to some new, bland duplexes and Frank came to a stop in front of one of them.

"This is it," he said, as he turned the car off and got out. Roman sat still.

"I'll just wait here."

"Man, come on in. These guys are cool. You'll like them. You're practically one of us now."

Frank knocked on the door. When it was opened Roman was hit first with the smell of dirty dishes, stale beer, cigarettes, and weed.

"Come on in," Gary said.

They stepped into the room. Roman remembered Gary from Junior/Senior and began to feel at ease. The TV was on and there were three couches. On each couch were two guys who looked older, slouched back, staring at the TV. They barely took notice of Roman and Frank. Roman noticed a water bong in the center of the coffee table, a bag of weed beside it, and beer cans on every table. The guys were all drinking. Surfboards were leaning in the corner beside a fish tank.

Gary went into the kitchen, took a shirt off one of the chairs, and put it on. He then slipped his feet into some flip-flops and walked back over to them. "You ready?"

Frank nodded and turned toward the door.

"Gary, this is Roman."

"We met at Junior/Senior," Gary said, turning around and holding out his hand.

Roman shook it.

"Again. Just remember," Gary was saying, "don't mention who got this for you."

"Don't worry about it. Can you get us a keg?" Frank asked, holding out a wad of money.

"A keg?" Gary said looking at it, "Shit, man, I thought you just wanted a case or something."

"Tonight's graduation and we're having a big party."

"Whose parents are out of town?"

"Nobody's. Tripp and Roman found this great place out in the woods. We're gonna have it there."

Gary agreed, and they were soon at the liquor store. The long-haired hippie clerk glared at them as he rang up the sale. Behind the store, the keg tub and tap were secured in the trunk. Frank then took Gary back to his duplex.

"Don't you two go drinking that all by yourself," he said, smiling through the window before turning to head up his walkway. As they drove past the farmland between the city and Coxville, Roman again felt anticipation building as they pulled up into the yard of the old house. There were already cars there. The sun was down and, in the west, there was only an orange sliver of light on the horizon.

Augustus was standing in the Liberty High School hallway for the last time, lining up to go out and be seated for the graduation ceremony. He was dressed in a sharp suit beneath a dark blue gown. He felt ridiculous. Others around him seemed perfectly happy in it. He put the cap on and blew the tassel again to get it out of his line of sight. Everyone was talking at once until a teacher came out and shushed them. It was time. He walked in a single file line, much like primary school days—only without the yellow painted line on the floor—behind the person he was to sit next to. He looked at the back of the head of the person he was following, trying to remember who it was. The procession walked silently by beige-painted lockers and doorways to empty classrooms. The school was always a foreign place after school hours, hollow and vast. He had looked for Tripp but had not seen him before they got in line. He went through one of the multiple glass doors to the outside and saw that it was going to rain. On toward the football field they marched, passing the bleachers where family and friends were sitting. Shouts rang out from people in the bleachers. Seniors in line waved to their families. Augustus looked for Hart and his mother, Sarah, but couldn't see them. The seniors were seated, and Augustus found himself in the middle of one half of a giant square of seniors. He felt claustrophobic. He looked around at his classmates. No one was saying anything, many were looking around just as he was. Augustus felt a sudden urge to flee. He turned around and looked again into the bleachers, finally spotting his parents up among the crowd. He could see his father talking intently to the man beside him. Hart was always talking. Out on the football field, in those neatly ordered chairs, Augustus turned back around and listened to the band play. He opened the program. *Pomp and Circumstance*, he read. No doubt.

On his right side was Daniel Farmer, the one he had followed, who had been in a few of Augustus's college prep classes. No sports. Beat-up old station wagon in the parking lot. He wondered where Daniel Farmer was headed after the summer. The community college, definitely. He didn't have to ask, and he wouldn't. It would sound like he was talking down to Daniel. Everyone knows where I'm going, Augustus thought, and it felt strange to know this. A baseball scholarship was a big deal, headline news. His father could afford to send him anywhere. Augustus didn't feel right about it. He tried to think of who was Daniel's best friend. Warren Bullock.

On Augustus' left was Melvin Foreman. Black guy. Tall and lanky. He had weightlifting with Melvin this year; they knew each other in passing, but that was it. They had never spoken.

"Melvin," Augustus said.

Melvin jumped, surprised to hear his name.

"What are you doing after high school?" Augustus asked.

"Military," Melvin said.

"Really? Which one?"

"Air Force. I'm going to be a pilot."

The principal was speaking now. Augustus was thinking he really shouldn't have gotten stoned that afternoon. He shifted in his seat. He felt like everyone was looking at him, but as he looked around he saw that everyone was looking forward, chin up, listening intently to the principal. He saw Tripp run down the aisle and pass between people to get to his empty seat. Light laughter could be heard. Augustus shook his head and caught Tripp's eye. Tripp smiled. Augustus looked at the program to find his name. He tried not to look at the stage. She was there: Nora was sitting up on the stage. She was valedictorian and had cords on her gown. His was plain. He looked around and saw others with hanging cords and wondered what they were for. Nora would be making a speech. He looked off toward the dark sky as the wind picked up. A few raindrops fell and a whisper went through the crowd. The principal made a comment and there was a ripple of laughter. The principal tried to hurry things along. A speaker got up, then another. The rain fell harder for a second and there was a slight stirring in the bleachers, but the rain subsided and the ceremony went on. Augustus wondered what would be going on tonight. He wondered what Nora would do. Would he see her? Finally, she got up and began her speech. Augustus felt like she was consciously trying not to look at him. He tried not to look at her, but he couldn't help himself. He wished he could have been with her at this moment and share her joy and triumph. She was better off, he thought, without believing it. She was radiant and he was happy for her and felt pity for himself. She was saying something that would never be heard when a gust of wind blew caps off heads. A flash of lightning streaked through the sky, and a boom of thunder rattled the crowd into a panic. They fled the bleachers. The seniors scattered as the rain poured down on them. Augustus stood up and saw Nora still at the podium, her gown soaked. They exchanged glances and, in that moment, shared a bereaved glance that neither of them would ever forget for the rest of their lives. Nora turned slowly and left the stage, her eyes cast downward. Augustus followed the rest inside. He didn't go to the gymnasium, where graduation was being reorganized, but walked out to the parking lot, possessed with malice toward the world. He got into his Corvette and tore out of the parking lot, almost losing control on the wet road, and the rain fell in his wet tire tracks, as if he had never been there.

Roman, Frank, and some other juniors were standing on the porch of the old house as the rain poured down around them and the wind swayed the branches and rattled the leaves of the tall oak trees. The fire they had started in the back yard was slowly being put out as Roman listened to the heavy drops drum on the metal roof of the house. The water flowed almost in a solid wall off the edge of the porch roof. He thought how soothing the sound was as he looked at the dour faces of his companions. The outlook for the party was getting bleak. No one said anything until the rain started to taper off.

"See, I told you," he heard someone say.

The keg had been moved up onto the porch. The rain clouds overhead moved into the west and left a damp presence as the buzzing sound of crickets resumed in the background. The revelers rallied and went back to their chairs and drinking. Roman sipped from his cup, listening to the conversations around him. They had come prepared; a truckload of stuff had been set up. There were folding chairs—beach and lounge chairs, even—everywhere. There was a cooler full of ice and several fifths of liquor with mixers and chasers. The beer bong had its own carrying strap from which it hung on a nearby tree limb.

Roman only knew Frank out of this group. Someone passed him a joint. He puffed on it—his buzz from earlier in the day had turned into a headache. These juniors, knowing that in a year's time they would be doing the same, were an anxious bunch. For them, this night was a warning. Roman was already feeling like a has-been. When you're in high school it's easy to know who, what, and where you are, he thought. After this night he wondered just who, just what, he would become. He was convinced back in Seaside he was already forgotten as the guy who moved away. Everyone became ultimately just a short declarative statement in the end. I'll be the "whatever happened to him guy," he thought.

More people showed up, filled cups, and joined the quiet banter of the night. Roman was starting to feel more comfortable and warmer as his buzz grew. Through the advance of this growing internal glow, he heard dozens of soft, inaudible conversations and the interspersed punctuation of laugher. He swatted at a mosquito that left an itchy bite on his ankle.

"Look," someone said and pointed.

Roman, filling up his cup, turned and saw the long streaming lines of paired glints in the dark. The line of headlights went as far as he could see. It was the seniors. Almost instantaneously, the small tribe grew into a sea of heads and cars. The house hung eerily as a backdrop to the entire scene. A few people stood on the steps and porch, other, sat, their legs hanging off the ledge. All had a beer and were enjoying themselves. From a forest to the left there were people scrounging for firewood. Roman watched them.

"Does anyone know who lives here?" someone asked.

The reply was, "I don't know."

"When they get home, they sure are going to be pissed."

Augustus pulled his Corvette off Nash Road and parked with some other cars. He had been by Gary's place to pick up the fifth of vodka Gary had promised him. He'd had three Screwdrivers before he left. He was still wet from the downpour at graduation, the cap and gown now wadded in the space behind his seats. He opened the cooler next to him and pulled out the orange juice and vodka. Get morbidly drunk was his plan and he took a straight gulp from the vodka bottle, got out, and walked toward the fire and silhouettes of people. Augustus said hello to some passersby he couldn't quite make out in the dark.

Augustus stepped up to the fire and nodded at Roman. Roman didn't know if Augustus remembered the night at Junior/Senior or if he was just embarrassed to bring it up. He had seen people get that drunk before and they never remembered anything. It's the type of drunkenness where you wonder if the person is going to die.

Augustus looked around and wondered if Nora was going to be there. Parties in the woods weren't her style. Once, when they were broken up, he had seen her trashed at a party and the way she acted horrified him. He could only stand a minute of her hanging on his shoulder, looking at him with those "you asshole" eyes yet smiling all the same, smelling of liquor.

"We need some fucking light out here," he said, and everyone agreed.

Nora could feel soreness in her legs that she knew came from being on her feet for so many hours. What a day, she thought. Saying goodbye to the teachers she had loved so much and those who had helped her. And then there was her family, who had come into town the night before. Her adoptive mother's sister and husband, two cousins she barely knew. The older she got, the more apparent it was to her that her family was a lie. It wasn't a bad lie; she knew they loved her as if she were their own, but a space between them was widening. She thought about Augustus and how much he had always wanted her to find out who her real mother was. If she did, would that betray her adoptive parents? It wasn't that she didn't have anything in common with her family, it was just so awkward for Nora around them.

Then there was everything else in the back of her thoughts—anxiety about the summer and the future. She had thought she and Augustus would make it to this day. She had always believed if they could just get out of high school things might go right for a change. She made excuses that it was the prearranged little world of high school that had always caused so many problems. If they could just get out of it, get free of the past and all the gossip, they would finally be able to do the things they had always talked about. Going to college together, getting married, having children. Be the couple everyone wanted to be around, like they had been before. She tried to push it all out of her mind but it was all there, it was just too much to push away. So she carried it with her everywhere she went.

"This is the place."

"Huh?" Nora snapped out of her reverie. "Can't we go somewhere else?" she asked.

"I want to see Tripp for at least a minute," Betty said.

"I can't see a house."

They got out and started walking down the road, past the cars lined up on both sides.

"There must be a lot of people here," Betty commented.

A truck turned out of a driveway and started coming toward them. The headlights bore down on them and then stopped. It was Frank.

"What are you two ladies up to?" he asked.

"Heading up to the party," Betty said.

"It's a rager, we're going to get another keg now," Frank said through Roman's window. Roman saw that it was Nora, and he froze. Nora looked from Frank to Roman and smiled.

"See you in a bit," she said.

The truck drove off and Betty and Nora continued walking. People were visible now.

"Who was that guy with Frank? He's been hanging out with Tripp a lot," Nora asked.

"He's the new guy from Seaside. His name is Roman."

"I met him Junior/Senior, but I didn't get his name. What year is he?'

"He's a senior."

"How long has he been at Liberty?'

"Two months."

"Why would anyone transfer in the last two months of high school?" Nora asked.

"You'll have to ask him that," Betty said. "It'll get your mind off Augustus."

It was dark, the sky had cleared, and the only light was from the full moon and the glimmer of a fire. The comet was still there high in the night. There were people everywhere, standing next to cars, sitting on the open beds of trucks, and anonymous bodies scurrying into the woods. Betty and Nora found their friends, who gave them cups to fill.

Through the flickering orange fire and the crowd of shadowy bodies, Nora saw Augustus clearly. To her, he still loomed larger than life. She looked away. Betty nodded her head over that way, but she realized Nora had already seen him. Nora shook her head, eyes grave.

Betty put her hand on Nora's arm. "I won't make you," she said.

The keg went dry without notice. Roman and Frank arrived soon after with the new keg and, before the truck had stopped, the keg had already been taken out of the bed, thrown into the tub of ice, and tapped.

"Jesus, you people are going to get run over," Frank shouted.

Roman spoke to a few new people he had met. The guys were all on a baseball team together and from the things they said they were pretty good. The whole time they spoke a joint was going amongst them.

To his right was a sullen fellow drinking slowly but steadily from a cup and every time it went empty, methodically, he disappeared and reappeared, cup refilled. His stare never left the fire. Further away on his left was Augustus, who watched curiously—both the fire and the house.

As the night turned cooler, they moved closer to the fire. Here, further from the river, Roman could feel the humid, grassy greenness of everything. The people around him started talking about Augustus's touchdowns and home runs. Another person chimed in about his batting average, the state title, and a university. Roman watched the subject of this conversation squirm in his lounge chair, looking embarrassed.

"Do you remember that game at…?"

"Over the fucking trees, man. I've never seen anything like it."

"Are you going to play both sports at State?"

Roman wondered when Augustus would say something.

"Who was that girl you dated? Man, she was so…"

It went on and on. Roman wished they would just shut up; he was beginning to feel a vague sympathy for their silent superhuman again. The mythic athlete, partyer, Lothario, whom he had to carry, wounded and weak, Junior/Senior weekend, and who had not spoken to him since. Augustus uttered nothing. Just stared into the fire. No bragging or boasting came from him. He just sat there as if he were not present. Roman expected him to join them at any moment and be carried away by his own inflated ego. Roman felt it was what they wanted: they would have accepted anything from him and hated him for it. In Roman rose a jealousy, a childish envy, that he couldn't explain. Roman had noticed he and Augustus were the same height, but Augustus looked bulkier. He reminded Roman of someone.

"I need a drink," their hero announced, breaking up their conversation, silencing them, as he reached in his cooler, pulled out the fifth of vodka, gulped down what remained of it, and left. Augustus had had enough.

"Hey, Augustus!" Tripp yelled from the porch, where he was standing with Nora and Betty.

Augustus didn't hear him. There were candles lit and lined up along the edge of the house's porch. The house looked decorated for Christmas, but the light let everyone see one another.

"Drunkass," Tripp mumbled. "Where is he going?"

"I think some people are going over to Tom's house," Nora interjected quickly, wanting to leave after seeing Augustus walk off. She still wished he would talk to her, but no good would come from that.

Betty looked at Tripp. "You ready to go?" she asked him.

Tripp looked around and back at Betty, then Nora, and could see that Nora wanted very badly to leave.

"Yeah," he said, "Let's go."

The hours rolled on and the night became a dark starlit carnival as the masses gathered, reached whatever heights they could, and drifted on to wherever they had to go. It was late, the party was done, and Roman felt heaviness behind his eyes. He was in a folding beach chair, legs crossed, drunk as hell, scattered cigarette butts around his feet, a half-full cup of beer in his hand, his mind exhausted. He was too drunk pass out, to move—to care about anything, really. The keg was floating in its trash can just behind him, the tap flung over the side in despair. There were a few laggards. Tripp and Frank were long gone. Some people were scattered in the yard, voices in the darkness, among the last of the parked cars. Some were still on the porch—its candles gone out—all now in total darkness, taking the last few breaths of the night. Around him, some guys he didn't know were still sitting, lounging, half-conscious, around the dying red embers of the fire. A call for more wood came from someone. Roman thought he heard something like a moan.

Most had gone home to their curfews. The hangers-on were an assorted array of newfound friends, bonded by the late hour. As they sipped the last of their cups and cans the main concern was what were they were to do now and how they could obtain more beer to keep the night alive, even though it was dead. None were in any condition to move, nor all that motivated to do so.

Roman's head was swirling when he saw headlights coming up the road. The guy who was next to Roman sat up. There were loud engines approaching. Two trucks came to a stop in the beaten-down grass, headlights bearing down on those still around the fire. The engines shut off and people got out, whooping and yelling.

"Damn," groaned the guy next to Roman.

"What is it?" Roman asked.

"Trouble. Rednecks. Just be cool. They trashed a guy's house a couple months ago."

"Why did they do that?"

"Shits and giggles. To start something."

Roman looked around and noticed that his companions all seemed a little more alert and tense. Roman knew guys like this back in Seaside.

The foursome, obviously drunk, walked up to the keg.

"Where's the beer?" one of them asked, picking up the tap and slinging it back down.

"It's gone," the guy next to Roman said. "Have you got any?"

Roman had never been in a fight. There were always certain guys in any class that got off on it. Usually, they would fight with others who they heard liked to fight. But every now and then some innocent would be inevitably trounced.

Augustus was awakened by the noise of engines. He had passed out on the far side of the house, in the grass, after throwing up. He got to his feet, feeling better, and walked around the house, hearing voices. Around the corner of the house, he looked at the four newcomers and he knew who they were. Wayne, Stacey, Ron, and Kyle. Augustus had heard the story of the house they trashed. It was the house of a girl he knew, a friend, and how he wished he had been there. He would have done something. It made him sick to think about whoever was just standing around watching that night. Augustus felt a furor and his legs and arms started to shake. It was an adrenaline rush he knew well from when he had been in fights before. He had been in two. No one really knew about them. One was when he got jumped at a college party when the people he went with left and he talked to some other guy's girlfriend. The other was when a friend had gotten into a fight and Augustus had intervened and ended up pummeling someone. He had felt bad about that one for a while. In the first fight he had taken quite a beating that, in the end, he strangely felt good about. Augustus crept close and crouched behind a parked car so he could listen. He saw them circling, like vultures, to see who would fall into their trap.

"Hey, fuckhead," Wayne said in Roman's direction. Wayne was the surliest of them, the instigator.

No one moved or said anything.

Wayne kicked Roman's chair. Roman turned and looked up at him.

"Hey, new guy, you got any beer?" Wayne asked.

"It's all gone," Roman said. He could feel himself tensing up, ready for what was coming. He would have to stand up to have any chance.

"What the fuck did you say?" Wayne asked abruptly.

When Augustus heard this, something went off in his head and he charged. Before Roman could reply, he saw Augustus come up to Wayne and swing his fist squarely into Wayne's nose with a soft crack. Blood flew out of Wayne's nose and his head snapped back and he fell to the ground. Roman jumped up, ready for one of Wayne's friends, but Augustus immediately went for Stacey. Augustus's blow hit his chin before he could even react. As Stacey stumbled back Augustus hit him in the stomach, Stacey fell to the ground, and Augustus kicked him in the head. Augustus then turned to the other two. Kyle and Ron came at him, but Augustus was too fast and punched Kyle in the face as he was grabbed from behind by Ron. Roman jumped up and grabbed Kyle, stunned by Augustus's blow, and wrestled him to the ground. Augustus turned and grabbed Ron and threw him to the ground and smashed his face with a kick. Then Stacey came at Augustus and hit him in the back of the head, but this only made Augustus mad. He turned and smashed Stacey's nose. Blood flowed again. Wayne got up and came at Augustus again, but Augustus dodged his fist and hit Wayne in the mouth. Wayne fell to the ground, knocked out cold. The others at the party jumped on Kyle with Roman while others started kicking Ron. Stacey held his mouth and backed away. Augustus called for a halt when all four were on the ground. They watched as Augustus went over to Wayne again, who was still on the ground. Augustus raised his fist, but Roman grabbed his arm. Augustus was breathing hard and Roman pulled him back. Roman let go of Augustus, who stopped and looked at the other two.

"You motherfuckers want some more?" Augustus shouted down at them. Ron and Kyle flinched. "Help them up," Augustus said. As they were being helped up, Augustus bent over them and yelled in their faces.

"Get the fuck out of here!" he said, kicking Wayne one more time in the stomach. Roman pulled Augustus back. "Come out here and try to ruin everyone's night? Our graduation? You think you're going to fuck up my night?"

Roman tried to calm Augustus down by putting his hand on his shoulder. The two who were badly beaten helped the other two stumble off into the darkness. Everyone beathed a sign of relief as the cars drove off. The was a hush as no one knew what to do. Augustus was pacing back and forth huffing and cursing under his breath. Roman started to try to say thanks, but Augustus did not see him as he stormed off, swearing at the night. Roman exhaled, sat back down in his chair, wiped sweat from his forehead, and looked at the others standing around the fire in stunned astonishment. He thought about the cruelty and menace that sometimes shows itself, but one thing was certain—Augustus had saved his ass.

EIGHT

Roman stirred. He rolled over onto his side, trying slip back into the affectionate oblivion of sleep. He could hear birds chirping and he tried to shut them out. He wanted more sleep, just a little more. There was a distinct whine of an approaching engine on the road just out his window. He listened as it got closer and closer. He rolled onto his back and stared at the ceiling, trying to fix an image and direction of the sound. He would listen to the cars at night, the familiar piercing swoosh of air as they approached and then faded away. In the morning, when the small town came to life, it was often hard to go back to sleep. Today was Saturday and there was nothing he had to worry about.

He lay there, thinking about the past night and the girls he had met. Wasn't there something about them that made everything better—less lousy? He tried to remember their names: Linda, Kim. The girl Frank talked to all night that he didn't like at all—she was too loud.

They had seemed to hang on his every word of what Seaside was like, the boats and the beach, what people did there. He left out the important parts, like Cassandra, and he started to feel guilt; it rose, snuck up on him. He'd had the dream about her again, the one he was afraid of having. In it he sees her, and she is angry, and he can't get sounds out of his throat no matter how hard he tries. Roman knew what that dream was all about. He had promised to call and he had not, had not gone back to see her as he had promised. He had not done anything he had said he would, and he felt rotten about it. He would call her later if he could gather up the courage. He just hadn't thought things would go so well here in Coxville.

Again, the guilt. He counted the days since he had last spoken to her and went back over every day since and what he had done, but it all seemed like a mad blast of faces. She had called at the end of May—it was now late June—and left a message on his answering machine. He imagined her hurt and winced at the thought. Calling her and telling her it was over was what he should do, but he was distracted by a rumbling that came closer and closer and then came to a stop. It was just outside. It couldn't be a lawn mower; they didn't have one. The grass in the yard needed cutting. The engine was, at intervals, being revved up. He went to the kitchen for a glass of water. He looked out the kitchen window and, beyond a tree, heard the distinctive baritone hum, and knew it had to be a car engine coming from his father's garage. Roman went to his room and threw on yesterday's smoky clothes and put on his sandals. He looked at the clock. Nine a.m.

Roman stepped into the sunlight, felt dingy, and knew it was going to again be hot, probably in the 90s. Weeks had passed since graduation night. The days all ran into one hazy flash of sun. He went back inside, to his room, and located his sunglasses. He went outside again and followed the small concrete walkway over to the old store and garage. He still thought the walkway odd, the way it ended just before it got to the station on the corner.

He looked into one of the open bays, where there was a black car he had never seen. The hood was up and Baron was hunched over the engine. The engine revved again, which startled him.

Roman looked around. There was a large industrial-sized fan blowing loudly from the corner. His father's tools were scattered about. There were empty quarts of oil everywhere and discarded boxes and the plastic that parts came wrapped in. Here and there an empty drink bottle, Styrofoam cups, a balled-up bag from some fast-food joint. In the other bay another car, a small, old four-door with its hood up and the engine dismantled.

Roman hadn't worked since graduation. His father hadn't asked him to come over and help nor had he insisted he get a job. He had not seen his father in a month, he had been so busy hanging out with his new friends.

"Hey!" Roman shouted over the engine.

Baron's head peeked out the side of the raised hood.

"Morning," Baron said in a gruff, serious tone, and he disappeared behind the raised hood.

Roman walked up to the front of the car, getting a good look at it. He had never seen anything like it. It was one of those old muscle cars. It struck him as odd, this car being in his father's garage. It was menacing. His father talked about cars all the time. But cars weren't thought of these days like they had been in the old days, like in the movies from his father's time when cars were everything.

"What kind of car is this?" Roman asked.

Baron stood up with a smile, grabbed a red rag, and started to wipe his hands off. Roman saw that his father was in his usual work attire—blue pants, belt, and gray shirt, all covered with the grease he hated so much. Baron walked around the car to the driver door, reached in, and turned the engine off.

"What?" he asked.

"What kind of car is this?"

Baron looked down at the car with a curious pride. "This…is a 1969 Ford Mustang Boss 429."

"This is a Mustang?"

"Yes."

The only idea in Roman's head was of the late-model Mustangs he had seen recently. A couple of people had the new Mustangs in Seaside. He remembered there had been a few he had seen around Martinsboro, too. People with Mustangs always had the tops down.

"I've never seen one like this."

"They're very rare. You don't see many at all."

"Whose is it?" Roman asked.

Baron looked at him, as if he had forgotten something. "It's mine."

Roman walked up closer to the black machine and peered through the open window into the interior. It smelled old.

"Is this what you have been working on all this time in here?" Roman asked.

"A lot of the time, I guess. People are coming in for oil changes and other things every now and then. I just had it painted. Got it back this morning."

"Where did you get it?" Roman asked.

"It was my father's," Baron replied.

Roman remembered the funeral they had attended briefly, at which they had stood in the back. He thought about asking his father about his grandfather, but he didn't. He just wanted to get out of there before his father started asking questions.

"I've got to meet some friends," Roman said. "Over at the country club. My friends Harrison and Frank are members."

Baron said nothing and Roman turned to leave.

"Roman!" Baron called out just as he was at the bay door

"Yeah?"

His father shook his head and looked down. Roman looked back for a second but when he realized his father had nothing more to say he went out, wanting to say something. He couldn't remember the last time his father had said his name.

Roman walked back to the house, discouraged. He realized—and he wondered how it had never occurred to him before—that there were a lot of things his father had not told him over the years. It now occurred to Roman that his father had a family here. He remembered he had asked about his father's family on several occasions and Baron had responded with silence. When he had asked, he always remembered a painful look on his father's face and, not wanting to see that emotion, never asked again. Roman had all kinds of theories. He had asked his mother about Baron's family years ago, but she had only said that it was something for his father to tell him about and she claimed not to know much.

What followed was another day of pleasure for Roman and his friends. For the last month, he had been on a perpetual holiday. Some of his new friends had part-time jobs they had to go to during the day. Most were going off to college in August and were using graduation and college as leverage against doing just about anything resembling work.

Every day of the week in June had offered up some recreation. Tripp was available every day, Frank worked half days at a car wash. A guy named Craig had a place at the river and a boat to go skiing and wakeboarding. Arthur had a place at the beach, which Roman took his surfboard down to, and a guy named Alex had a pool in his backyard and a fake ID he got using his brother's birth certificate to buy alcohol. And there was always Gary's place in Martinsboro, over by the university; he was always home and always had weed for sale. But for the most part, with the students gone, the city was for the locals.

From late August to May Martinsboro swelled with more than twenty thousand students. The traffic increased, the energy of the city rose, but during the summer there was a lethargic absence of life in the city.

In Martinsboro and Coxville, summer was for the high schoolers—basketball games in the driveway, cutting your parent's grass, and baseball. At the recreation fields, men's and women's church softball, Little League, Babe Ruth. Baseball and softball were played nightly underneath the tall field lights. Mondays through Fridays the lights were visible for miles, along with the sounds of cheering at the sporting assemblies. Mothers, fathers, sisters, and brothers gathered on those silver bleachers. The local

American Legion team provided the Martinsboro elite a place to gather at the university's grand stadium, many of its players moving on to play at colleges and a few waiting to be drafted. In Martinsboro, baseball was king. Fountain Pepsis, popcorn, kids chasing foul balls for Blow Pops, and the smells of hot dogs, cut grass, and leather.

On dusty, solemn days as the grasses grew tall, the air took on a heavy humidity. The old white house on the river had become the summer mecca. Isolated and just outside of town, every night it drew visitors looking to see if anything was going on. Nightly, on weekdays, a few people would go down the long, deserted road and turn into the dirt driveway to smoke a joint or drink. The weekends were official and different. There had been a keg there every Friday or Saturday night since graduation. The first party on graduation night had mainly been Liberty seniors and juniors. The last two weeks, word had spread to the Scott High crowd. Cops were expected at any minute, it was part of the peril, but they hadn't come yet. The great summer secret was still safe, for now.

The humid June day slipped into a dark, starless blanket of night. The house was unlocked, so some of the early arrivals had migrated inside. The house had been completely empty originally, but soon beach chairs, tables, and stolen pool lounge chairs had been brought in, along with candles. In some of the rooms, people wrote on the walls. Someone with some skill had painted a mural. It was a replica of the barn out back and the view looking out at the backyard that led down to the river.

It was 9 p.m. and the sun slipped out of sight. A fire was started. Augustus walked back to his chair and sat down with a group of friends from Liberty, his back to the river, watching the cars park and their occupants pop out and join the party. Augustus looked around and chugged his beer.

"You know where any weed is?" Mike was asking a short, dark-haired guy on his right.

"Nah, man."

Augustus listened to the conversations around the fire and wondered why Mike could possibly want any more weed. A headache was forming in Augustus's head from smoking it all day.

"Scott is taking over this place," Augustus said.

"I thought those people were your friends, didn't you invite them?"

"No one's parents are out of town, I guess. So they're all coming out here," Mike remarked.

"Mike. You're staying here and going to college, right?" Keith asked.

"That's the plan."

"Why don't you go somewhere else?"

"I don't drive a Corvette," Mike said, sarcastically.

"Fuck you, Mike," Augustus said, smiling, "and you know what? I can't play the infield. I need another. You?"

Mike shook his head no

Scott people. Augustus knew them but had not invited them. He was surprised they were showing up. He had pissed a lot of people off when he quit Legion baseball, which was comprised of Scott people. Scott people had resented him from the start. They all were punks anyway. Augustus walked toward the woods to piss. He looked up at the comet and found no moon. Augustus saw that it was going to be a dark night and tried to forget about Scott. He was bored. He figured he should be happier than this, more excited about the future, but here he was at this same place again. When he thought about his future, all he saw was oblivion. His father was angry every day since he'd quit Legion baseball. The love of the game had just gone. It seemed silly to him now. It seemed phony.

Augustus felt a cool breeze and listened to the tall old trees around the house and along the river sway back and forth. For a moment, they drowned out the steadily increasing noise of the party. Cars could be heard coming to a stop out on the road, doors slamming. Laughter and talking. People were walking up the gravel drive in droves now. The crowd had swelled, everybody moving in the darkness. There were candles lit in every window and the wraparound porch was bursting with bodies.

Augustus saw someone running toward the old wooden dock. People sitting on it got out of his way as the runner hurled himself into the river. Everyone on the dock followed. Augustus walked up to the back of the house and climbed the steps up to a larger square porch area off the back of the house. He wondered when the house had last been lived in. There were people he knew everywhere; he didn't have to say anything to anyone right off. The chatter had become louder as Augustus looked over at a beer bong being raised.

"Three fucking beers, man. That's fucking crazy!" someone shouted.

Augustus rubbed his forehead and face eyes trying to figure out just what was it all for. He felt only a vague connection to the masses. Like the comet overhead, he felt lonely and distanced. There was an exaggerated laugh to his left; Augustus turned but couldn't tell who it was. Off the porch to his left a pickup truck was backing up; a new keg was being brought by some juniors. The deck crowd applauded its arrival with a sense of renewed vigor and relief. An empty keg meant fun had to be sought elsewhere; an empty keg was a party's death.

"He wants to get it by himself," Augustus heard someone say.

The keg would not budge, and general laughter went around. A second junior went to help, and in seconds the crowd parted like the Red Sea and the new keg was installed. The crowd let Augustus fill his cup first.

Augustus thought he would see what the party inside was up to. He looked in; the kitchen and beyond was packed with bodies illuminated by candles on the windowsills. The music was coming from the living room. Someone had brought a strobe light. Everyone was dancing. Augustus pushed his way through arms and shoulders. It was hard to tell who anyone was. He brushed up against a girl he had never seen. He just stood there as she kept dancing up beside him. Augustus stopped and danced with her a minute. She took his cup of beer and drank from it. He smiled at her and moved away. There were people inside he knew of, from Scott, Harrell, and Franklin, whom he had seen before but never partied with. They just nodded to him as he passed. In the corner he noticed a group of last year's seniors, in college now but home for the summer, he guessed. One, a guy he knew, threw a hand up and waved to him. Tommy Jones had played baseball with him. Augustus nodded back and raised his cup as a sort of salute. The college group did the same back to him. He reached the front hallway and was finally free of the crowd. The front door was wide open. Out on the porch was mainly the Scott crowd.

A group of girls he had met through Nora cast sideways glances at him. Augustus could feel the judgment. He started to walk over to them, to convince them he wasn't a jerk. He wondered what Nora might have told them. There were so many things they had shared that wound up being talked about after a nasty break-up, half-truths and lies. He knew decent people were capable of vicious lies if they felt they were being betrayed. He had said nothing bad to anyone about Nora since they broke up; there was nothing really bad to say about her. Augustus, on the other hand, didn't like the thought of being talked about. He saw Logan sitting on the porch rail on the right. Augustus went over, thinking about the girl he had just danced with.

"Great party, man!" Logan said. Augustus just nodded, trying to figure out whether Logan was being sarcastic or not. He was the king of sarcasm. Augustus felt that, however he said it, even with that snobby tone of his, he was fine just where he was.

"Yeah, I guess," Augustus said, looking over at a group of girls on the porch drinking from cans of beer.

"You drinking from the keg?" Augustus asked.

"Nah, brought my own beer," Logan said, looking into the open front door of the house.

Augustus watched a group of senior girls from his class exit the front door and join the other girls on the porch. It looked strange to him, seeing Liberty girls with Scott girls.

"Hey, you're not going to go psycho tonight, are you?" Logan asked.

"No, not tonight," Augustus said.

"I heard you kicked the crap out of four rednecks."

"I was drunk. I don't really remember."

"I heard they were out here to look for you."

Augustus eyed him.

"Dude, I'm just fucking with you. You should have seen your face."

Augustus shook his head and lit a cigarette.

"Where are the rest of you Scott pricks?"

"Who are you talking about?"

"Those Legion punks."

"Did you really quit Legion? I never heard of anyone quitting Legion. Especially someone who started."

Augustus was feeling bold now.

"I did," he said.

The two paused to look the place over. Some other guys joined the pair on the porch. Augustus listened to Logan's stories for a while. He lit a cigarette and drank one of the beers handed to him. Augustus just shook his head as Logan and his entourage moved into the house to look for girls to talk to. Augustus wasn't in the mood. He was at the party, but he wanted to be alone. He stood on the steps looking up into the dark night sky. There was no moon, only the comet. There were waves of people still coming up the drive. Headlights came to a stop, dust swirled up in them, and bodies poured out of the cars. So many people.

"This is the biggest fucking party of the year," Augustus heard someone say over his shoulder. He took another sip from his beer.

"Can I bum a smoke?"

Augustus recognized the voice. He turned and gave Kelly Largo a frown. He handed her a cigarette.

"What's up, sport?"

"Don't call me that, Kelly," he said.

She smiled, knowing she still could get to him, could still frustrate him. Augustus tried not to look at her. She moved her head around in front of his, trying to catch his eye. Augustus was embarrassed around her still. He had made peace with what had happened between them. Kelly was one of the coolest, most beautiful girls at Scott, but she was a liar, and she had made a fool of him. At Liberty she might have been as unusual as Nora, but at Scott she was lost in a sea of rich, beautiful girls.

Kelly was alluring, mysterious, exotic. A lot like Nora in many ways, which was what drew him to her. Her father was from Casablanca and a doctor at the hospital. Her family was well-off. She lived in one of the fashionable neighborhoods with big houses, her mother the beautiful stay-at-home mom. She always wore the tightest clothes—showing off. Kelly was hot, and the worst part was that she knew it. She had a renegade charm and an adorable smile. You just knew that Kelly would always get everything she wanted. Augustus figured her destined for modeling or celebrity.

He was smitten with her the first night they met, and he knew from the first moment, the first time they kissed, that he was making a huge mistake. He just couldn't help himself. He was desperate to get over Nora. If only Kelly had fewer options. She had the worst reputation, as far as sexual history went, and Augustus tried to ignore the stories he heard about her. He knew the lies people were capable of telling to make themselves seem cool, no matter who was hurt. Last summer, when he and Nora had broken up, he had started hanging out with Kelly.

Augustus would pick her up in his flashy Corvette and take her to a party, and she would flirt with every guy there. He began to believe she encouraged rumor and liked the attention. He would watch her, his jealousy rising. He wanted to get mad at her, but that was what she had wanted. She toyed with him, mocking his old-fashioned values. It only led to humiliation. And one night when they were supposedly a "couple," he wandered into a bathroom and found her making out with some guy. He tried to think of it as her loss but couldn't distract himself from the suspicion that it was he who had lost something. An innocence, for sure, his belief in his own invulnerability, trampled by a girl who had casually dismissed him. He hadn't spoken to her since that party last summer, over a year ago. The whole episode had sent him back to Nora. Nora, whom he could trust to love him. Nora, who took him back. She always did, and he always felt a renewed sense of purpose.

Many had reveled in Kelly's dalliance with him, he imagined. They enjoyed watching him suffer and cheered as Augustus's arrogant adventures unraveled day after day. She brought him down a notch. Augustus the romantic, with an entirely obsolete code, in the last decade of the twentieth century. He was so out of step with his time.

Luckily, there were a great many other things going on that summer and the whole thing was forgotten, except by Augustus. After getting back with Nora, they dated for eight good months. Augustus thought he had been cured of his failure but, as always, he became restless again. So here he was now, drunk every night, but not drunk enough right now. Kelly took a sip from her beer and then took a drag from her cigarette. Augustus thought about being nice, with the idea of trying to hook up with her, but he remembered too strongly the past and could not bring himself to try it. All he had was his pride, after all. It was just too damned bad.

"How are things?" he asked.

"I heard you and Nora broke up, *again*," she said, this last word with such emphasis that he knew she was mocking him. He let it go and nodded. He liked her—he hated her—he could see himself loving her. He took another drink and lit a cigarette.

"What guy are you making a fool of now?" he struck back.

"What's it to you?"

"Just concern for my fellow man."

Kelly smiled insincerely and sighed, turning the conversation back to a friendly joke. "No one in particular. No one comes close to you."

Augustus nodded and looked her and paused. "Take care of yourself, Kelly," he said quickly and turned and walked back to the house.

"Augustus!" she called after him, but he ignored her and decided to get the hell out of there. There was the past, and then there was the past within the past. The failures from the efforts to move on, to do the right thing. Those are the failures that never truly heal, they are just lived with, and those memories of failure creep up in the middle of the day sometimes. The hope is that something was learned, and, just maybe, life would be better.

NINE

Tripp slowed the car as he and Roman tried to determine just what was going on at Nora's house. They turned on to Jones Street and saw a few cars parked alongside the road and in the driveway. Roman looked for movement as best he could through the lit windows. Tonight would be the third night Nora's parents had been out of town; Tripp and Frank had been there the last two nights, while Roman had stayed home. The whole summer he had spent almost every night at Frank's house, or Tripp's, or wherever they ended up. Each night's adventure delivered the crew to a different house—wherever parents were out of town. They cruised the roads, stopped by the abandoned house by the river, or went to apartments near the university where Tripp and Frank knew people in college.

Nora's house was large and well-lit among the sleeping, darkened monoliths of the neighborhood.

"Pull in here," Frank ordered.

"Dude, I'm doing the driving."

The Honda came to a crooked stop, one tire still on the road. Tripp, Roman, and Frank got out and walked up to the house. Overhead, bugs were swarming in the floodlights.

"Who's up here?" Roman asked in a whisper.

"That's Logan's car and that one is Victoria's," Tripp said, "and you don't have to whisper."

"So, where is everybody?" Frank asked, blowing out his last puff of smoke and flicking the butt. Roman saw it land in Nora's yard.

"She didn't want to have a party," Tripp answered, "just a few friends over."

They climbed the steps. The door was unlocked, so they went in. Logan, Jimmy, and Landon were in the kitchen when they came in.

"What's up, guys?" Logan asked.

"Who's here?" a voice from the next room asked.

Logan answered, "It's Tripp, Frank, and some guy."

Logan turned to Roman and held out his hand. "What's up?"

"I'm Roman."

"Logan."

Roman shook hands with the rest of them and followed Tripp into the living room. He looked up at a clock on the wall. It was 9:30. Moving through the group of guys in the kitchen Roman heard voices in the living room. He went in. Betty was sitting on the floor, staring intently at her playing cards. She pretended not to notice as Tripp went behind her, knelt down, and kissed her on the cheek. Roman stood, trying not to look as awkward as he still felt sometimes. He knew these people, had partied with them, yet still felt a hesitancy.

"Can't you see I'm concentrating?" Betty insisted, pushing Tripp away.

"Get a room," Nora remarked, shaking her head and catching a glimpse of Roman standing behind the couch.

Roman leaned against the doorway and crossed his arms. Nora, in a yellow sundress, sat on the floor, her back to the brick fireplace hearth. She was sitting cross-legged, looking at her cards, her mouth slightly open, as if deciding some strategy. Roman tried to make eye contact. He knew she was ignoring him. He felt nervous and could feel his heart pounding. Putting his hands in his pockets to seem more nonchalant, he tried to figure out an opening to get closer to her. Roman was ruminating about the times he had seen her before. He had never seen her at school. There was the first time he saw her, on the beach during Junior/Senior weekend, and the graduation night party. When he looked back at the people in the kitchen, they were all looking at him.

"Do you want to play?" Nora suddenly asked him. Roman, stunned, pointed at himself, a question on his face.

"What are you guys playing?" he asked.

"Asshole."

"Let me get a beer," Tripp said.

"Drink five," Nora said. "What about you?" she asked, looking up at Roman.

"I'm not drinking," Roman answered.

"Then you can't play," Nora said with a small smile and looked back at her cards. Tripp came in from the kitchen and handed Roman a beer.

"You are now," Tripp said with a wink.

Logan, Frank, and Jimmy were still in the kitchen assessing the beer situation.

Roman took the beer grudgingly. Nora looked up at him and nodded for him to come over. He went over and sat down on the floor between Betty and Tripp with Nora directly across from him.

"Do you know how to play?" Betty asked.

"I've seen it played," Roman responded.

"Christ, where are you from, anyway. Drink, Valerie," Betty said.

Roman didn't get a chance to answer.

"Drink for not knowing how to play," Valerie said to Roman.

"I'll show him," Betty added, giving Nora a look.

A few hands were dealt, seats were changed, and rules against cursing were made. Roman finished his third beer and was beginning to feel warm and happy. The game was paused for a smoke, and they got up to go outside. Roman followed Nora and they stood outside, smoking in the cool night air. Tripp and Betty held each other close. Roman and Nora stood awkwardly apart, looking around and trying to think of something to say.

"I've seen you before," Nora said finally after a long pause. "It was at the graduation party."

"And at the beach. Junior/Senior weekend," he added. Roman heard a snicker from Tripp, who had gone with Betty into the screened-in porch. Nora looked up at the stars. Roman leaned back against the porch rail.

"So, how has it been being the new guy?" Nora quipped.

"Do you have to call me that?" he asked.

"I'm sorry, it's just everyone's talking about you and not me. You could say I'm a bit jealous. I'm an only child so I like being the center of attention."

Roman looked down, embarrassed.

"So, you're already tired of being the new guy?"

"You could say that."

"I was the new person at one time myself."

"Is that right?"

There was a long silence. "So, I hear you're from the beach," Nora said finally.

"I'm from Seaside. That's where I've lived my whole life, but I sorta think my dad is from here."

"What makes you think that?"

"Just some little things. My dad seems to know a lot of people here. He works over in a shop that I think he's worked in before. I don't know, it just seems weird. There's a lot he's not telling me about."

"That is strange."

"Yeah, tell me about it," Roman said. "I'm sorry. I don't mean to get so serious."

Nora nodded. "I'm not from here either. I moved here in fifth grade from up north," she said.

"I knew there was something different about you."

Nora shifted and crossed her arms. "So, what do you think of Martinsboro?" she asked.

"It's been cool so far. I've met a lot of really cool people."

The girls from inside came out on the deck to smoke a cigarette and tell Nora that more people were there. Roman kept quiet and tried to blend into the night. When he went back in the house had filled with newcomers, the stereo was cranked, and the party Nora didn't want to have had begun.

Augustus was drinking in John's kitchen and looked at the fifth of vodka he was putting a major dent in. It was half gone. He looked at the clock. Only thirty minutes had passed. He started to mix another drink when he decided to try a sip from the bottle. He barely tasted it. Someone came in and said they were leaving.
"You coming, Augustus?" Ryan asked.
"Why the hell not?" He finished off his drink, then grabbed the vodka and the rest of his orange juice and headed outside. A commotion was going on around a car parked in the drive; many more bodies than the car could carry were trying to get in it.
"We can do this," Augustus said.
They crammed in to shrieks of laughter and jostling elbows and knees. Three in the back seat had two in their laps. Augustus was in the middle and was squished, but he was toasted and didn't give a damn. A girl's face was close to his and he could smell her makeup. He felt the other girl's breast on his arm and her hair, smelling of shampoo, was in his face. He peeked through a space between heads and saw a girl was on the lap of the front passenger, who he couldn't make out, and someone was driving; John, he thought. Augustus got an arm free and took a sip from the vodka bottle.
"He's not even mixing it anymore," someone said.
"That's an open container. If we get stopped, we're fucked."
"Relax."
Augustus burped.
"That's disgusting."
"That stank."
Augustus laughed.
"This many people in a car is fucking crazy."
"Let me drive," Augustus said.

"You can't drive. You're wasted."

"Let the man drive if he wants to."

"I drive better when I'm drunk," Augustus said.

"That's the dumbest thing I ever heard."

"Fuck you, whoever you are. I'm sober."

"Let him drive."

"You're sober, all right."

"Might I ask where this clown car is headed?" Augustus asked.

"Nora's having a party."

"Nora? I can't go there. Let me out."

"You buy the ticket, you take the ride."

"No, see, I really can't go there."

"You guys broke up, what, four months ago? I think you can safely be around her now."

"You think so?"

"I know so."

Augustus was too drunk to argue. When they let him out, he would just walk down to someone else's house. The radio was blasting as the car careened down the road. Everyone was talking at once. He took another sip and the car braked hard at a stoplight.

"What's your name?" Augustus asked the girl on his lap.

"Colleen," she said.

"Can I get a kiss, Colleen?" Augustus asked.

"Maybe later," she said, smiling.

"I might not be around later."

"Then maybe you should stick around."

The girl's tailbone was digging into his leg now and it hurt. God, please let me survive, he prayed.

Nora was taking tequila shots in the kitchen. She slammed the shot glass down on the counter and felt the burn in her throat. The house was full of people.

"Nora's getting drunk," she heard someone say, and hearing it sent a rush through her. She took another shot.

"Somebody needs to watch her."

"We need music," Nora said, and went into the living room and pulled down some CD cases. She flung the ones she didn't like on the floor.

"Here's one."

She put in the Cowboy Junkies' "Sweet Jane" and turned up the volume. She started to sway to the music. Other girls came in and danced with her. Suddenly, she said, "This sucks," and changed it to some dance music and started grooving. More girls came in with drinks in their hands and started dancing. The coffee table was moved, and the living room became a dance floor. Nora stumbled back into the kitchen. Logan was there with the tequila.

"You ready for another?" he asked.

"And another and another and another…" she said, taking the shot glass and knocking the drink back.

Augustus forgot about his plan to walk away when he saw all the people and cars. The vodka was hitting him, and he could barely see. He had tunnel vision now, it was like looking through a peep hole. The night felt worn, old, used up. Augustus went up to Nora's house, which had an almost unrecognizable quality to it, as if he was seeing it for the first time. He went in the front door and knew he had to piss. He moved through people and reached the bathroom. While he relieved himself, he saw his reflection in the mirror. The person looking back at him appeared both angry and tired. He splashed water on his face and dried off. He went in the kitchen, felt hot and, not wanting to talk to anyone, went back out the front door and stood on the porch. He remembered the vodka he was still clutching, took a sip, and caught a delirious glimpse of Kelly Largo. She was standing with a group on the front lawn. He staggered over and stood beside her.

"What's up, love of my life?" Augustus said and put his arm around her.

"Ah…Augustus, you're wasted."

Augustus felt woozy

"Are you all right?" Kelly asked.

Augustus leaned into her. "Kelly. Do you remember that night…"

Nora walked up to the two of them, "What are you doing here?" Nora screamed and pushed him. Augustus staggered back, tripped, and fell to the ground. Nora jumped on top of him, her hands swinging at his head.

"You fucking asshole! Fuck you! Fuck you! Fuck you!" Nora screamed.

"Kelly, help me." Augustus cried, not knowing what was happening.

Tripp, Frank, and Betty pulled Nora off him, but they couldn't hold her. Logan stepped in to help as they dragged her back. Some guys grabbed Augustus, who was now swearing and trying to get at her. They had to raise Nora, still in a frenzy, lifting her off the ground as she kicked and screamed. Augustus was pulled back, taken to a car, and put in the back seat.

"I'll get him out of here," Scott said.

Augustus lay in the back seat and everyone relaxed when, suddenly, he sprang up, found the door latched, opened it, and rolled out into the ditch. They put him back in the car and Scott drove away.

Augustus yelled out the open window, "I'll be baaaacccckkkkk!"

They took Nora back into the house and put her in the bathroom. She vomited for twenty minutes. Roman was on the back porch when Tripp came up to him.

"Man, I just saw the weirdest shit ever." Tripp said, "Nora just beat the shit out of Augustus."

"Why did she do that?"

"Man, who knows."

"Where is she?"

"She's up in her bathroom, puking."

Roman went up the stairs to the third floor. He was in Nora's room. He went into the bathroom and saw her sitting on the floor, her hands holding her hair back.

"I feel like shit," Nora said.

"You've looked better."

"Did you see what happen?"

"No, I was out back. Are you all right? What was that all about?"

"Augustus is an ass. We used to date."

Roman nodded.

"I'm fine now. It's over. Are you still interested?"

"Yes," he said.

"I'll let you take me out. I want to go somewhere nice."

"We can do that."

Roman helped her up and they went downstairs. Most of the partygoers had cleared out.

"Where were we earlier?" Nora asked

"I don't remember."

"All I've heard all summer has been all about you, with the Roman this and the Roman that."

He smiled and looked away into the night sky and the next yard. Nora went and sat on the top step and he sat down beside her. Roman was very close to her now. They were looking at each other and had nothing to say.

"Stay here," she said "I'll go get us another beer."

"You sure you want one?"

"I need one," she said.

Nora went in as Tripp came out.

"We're going to bed. Is she all right?"

"She's fine."

"You gonna take care of her?" Tripp said, smiling.

Roman nodded, and Tripp went inside. Nora came back and they went into the screened-in porch and sat on the porch swing.

"What's Seaside like?" Nora asked, holding her legs in tightly to her chest.

"You're cold."

"I'm fine."

"I'll get you a blanket."

Roman got up and went in the living room. He found an afghan on one of the couches, took it out to Nora, and draped it around her shoulders.

"A southern gentleman," Nora said sarcastically.

Roman shrugged. "I was brought up kind of old-fashioned."

"From my experience that means you went to church a lot."

"Yeah. I used to go with my father every Sunday, back home."

"You still haven't told me about home. I mean, you must have had friends you left behind, maybe even a girlfriend."

Roman was stunned for a moment. And realized there was a lot he had not thought about that he should have.

"Hey," Nora said, "you okay?"

Roman turned and looked at Nora again. "It's a lot like here, I guess. I played soccer. I worked with my father after school in his garage. Went to the beach every chance I got. I surfed a lot."

"What about your mother?"

"She left."

"When?" Nora asked.

"A year ago."

"What happened?"

"She took a job in Bloomsbury."

"We don't have to talk about it if you don't want to."

"No. It's fine, I just don't want to bum you out with my sad story."

"Our sad stories make us who we are."

"You're the first person I've mentioned it to here."

Roman felt guilt and surprise. He had held on so long to his grief, he had kept his secret until now. He felt he had said too much.

"What do you want out of life?" Nora asked.

"I don't know, at this point."

"You don't know, or you don't want to tell me?"

Roman shrugged.

"I really want to know," Nora pressed.

"You tell me first," he said

"You know, same things as everyone else."

"That's not an answer."

"I guess, fall in love," she said, quietly trying to make the word seem real.

"That would be a nice thing to happen," he agreed.

Nora leaned back and sighed.

"Where are your parents?" Roman said, trying to change the subject.

"They went up north to see my mother's twin sister."

"When are they coming back?"

"You don't want to talk about love?" she asked.

"No. Not really."

"Why not?"

"Because it's confusing."

"Maybe some other time," she said.

"That would be better."

"I'm really going to have to do a lot of cleaning tomorrow," Nora said quickly.

"They'll still know you had people over. There's always some beer can stashed somewhere that they find."

"Yeah, but they don't care if I have people over, they just don't want me to have any big parties."

Nora and Roman sat and talked for a while longer watching the heat lightning in the western sky. The sky immediately overhead grew darker and the clouds obscured the stars.

Upstairs in one of the bedrooms there was only a small lamp on the table beside the bed. Tripp was in his shorts with his shirt off, straining to peek through the blinds. Betty lay on the bed, flipping through channels on the TV.

"You're never going to find anything on at this hour," he said, perched on the ledge beneath the window. "Besides, the show is outside."

"Do you think we'll have a house like this one day?" Betty asked.

Tripp turned, not listening. "What?"

"What are you doing?" Betty asked.

"What does it look like?"

"Are you spying on them?"

Tripp smiled and started to laugh. "Yeah, I'm looking right at them."

"What are they doing?"

"They're just talking. God. People are so boring."

Tripp went back to the bed and lay down beside Betty. They cuddled up to each other, her head on his chest.

"What could they possibly be talking about for all this time?" Tripp wondered.

"Remind you of anybody?"

"Who?"

"Us. The first night we hooked up. You kept jabbering on and on. I thought you would never shut up and kiss me."

"Why, you no-good–" he started to tickle her. As she began to writhe and cackle, he tickled her even more viciously. Betty laughed harder and harder.

"Stop!" she screamed, "stop!"

"All right, all right."

"You know I hate being tickled."

"Oh, shut up. You love it."

"Do not!"

"Do too."

"Do not."

"You sound like you're in first grade."

"You sound like you're in first grade," she mocked him in a childlike voice.

"That's it. I've had it with you!" Tripp crawled on top of her and held her wrists. Betty tried to throw him off by lifting her legs.

"That's it, ride 'em, cowboy, yeaaah."

"Get off me!"

"Struggling will only make you tired."

Betty stopped struggling.

"Please stop," she said, as sheepishly as possible.

Tripp shook his head no.

"I'll have sex with you," she said.

"You'll do that anyway."

"If you don't get off me by the time I count to three, you'll never get it again."

Tripp smiled.

"One. I mean it."

"Sure, you do."

"Two."

Tripp began to laugh again.

"Thr-"

He jumped off her and rolled over beside her

"You know what you are?" Betty asked him.

"A brute," Tripp said.

"How did you know what I was going to say?" she asked, dismayed.

"I just know."

They lay in the dim light of the room. Tripp picked up his beer and finished it. They could hear the indistinct sound of voices from just outside the window.

"You're a bastard," Betty said.

"I love you."

"Oh, shut up."

"Did you tell him about Nora and Augustus?" Betty asked.

"No."

"Why not?"

"That's not up to me. It's up to her. I like Nora, and Augustus has put her through hell. I want to see her move on."

"Are you just saying that because that's what I want you to say?"

"No."

"Look. I like Roman. He seems to be a nice guy. If they like each other, that's up to them," Tripp said.

"Augustus is an asshole, anyway. He could never make up his fucking mind," Betty added.

"He's not an asshole. He's just … I don't know … flaky, sometimes."

"I'm getting tired." Nora said.

"Yeah, it's getting late."

Nora and Roman got up to go inside. He stopped and looked at one of Nora's family photos sitting on the bookshelf.

"What is it?" Nora asked.

"You look a lot like your mother."

"I can't. I'm adopted."

"I didn't know. I'm sorry."

"Don't worry about it. My mother and I do sort of favor," she said with a smile.

Roman was about to ask her more when he looked and saw that she had disappeared, and he heard her footsteps heading up the stairs. He lay down on the couch and stared at the ceiling. He was afraid he had made some grave mistake somewhere and it would undo everything.

Tripp came downstairs and got him up. They rode home with the windows open, smoking cigarettes in the silence of the predawn light. The ride home felt endless and dreamlike, the stars blinking in the warm night air. Tripp wanted to interrogate his friend; he was happy for him but felt the need for silence. They said nothing to each other as they rounded the curves and waited at stop lights, the only sound the clicking and blinking of the signal. Tripp smiled, remembering the feeling of when he knew Betty was the girl for him. Roman stared out the window. He was already in love and had been since he had first seen her.

Tripp dropped him off and he walked up to the steps of his house. It was one of those few nights in a lifetime without a final thought. The comet was there, high above the ethereal clouds of a coming storm, and he went in.

TEN

Baron sat in his car parked at the curb in front of the house he and Ann had shared in Seaside with the windows down, the hot sun shining in through the windshield, the radio turned down so he could barely hear it playing—the local oldies station—and wondered if he should just drive away. Something, way back in his mind, told him, urged him, that that was what he should do, but just once more—he had to know, had to feel it. He leaned his head back against the headrest and thought about when he was younger and a smoker, and that this was when he would have smoked, but now he didn't so, he simply sighed deeply. Baron wanted this over quickly.

He and Ann had picked this house out together. She was a TV anchor at the local station and a part-time journalist for the paper. From she made more money than he did as service manager at the Ford dealership. He could have made more money, he guessed, in sales or doing something besides running a garage and hunting and fishing all the time. He loved cars and the outdoors. He could have used his business degree at any time, but before he knew it, he just felt too old to start fresh. When he and Ann had met in college, he probably looked like he was headed one day to steady hours, working in a shirt and tie, even a suit, and maybe Ann was disappointed in him, that he hadn't done so, and he had slowly realized that she might be embarrassed by him.

Twenty years before, he had left Coxville for college in Seaside and had never looked back, so frustrating were his thoughts of home. Sure, he thought about going back, but he had made his own life for himself, and he was happy with it. But his father's death and Ann's leaving gave him good reasons to return and, besides, he had nowhere else to go. He was finally forced, by circumstances, to go home.

Being back in Coxville, he was happy—he was home. It wasn't as he had hoped, but the change had helped him get his mind off Ann. Now, middle-aged and able to support himself and Roman, he had everything to be grateful for. He had done everything he set out to do. He had married, had a lot of good years—though that was over, now—and had a son. But what had been the price of the independence in which he delighted? He had removed himself from the burden of his father's constant glare. But now that he was home and his father gone, he realized that had all been in his head. He felt selfish for not going home more, to see his family, to let Roman know them. He wanted for Roman what he had wanted for himself: he wanted Roman to live his own life, live his own dreams, and not be saddled with all-consuming family expectations. He didn't want Roman to have that feeling of working for family, and their approval, as he had. Just before Roman had been born he had considered going back, but he knew Ann wouldn't agree. Baron had called his father the night Roman was born, and his father said everything would be all right if he just came back home. But he didn't, and his father had been right, everything turned out fine. But now he wished Roman had known his grandfather.

Baron got out of the car and went up to the house. He unlocked the door and went in. He roamed the empty rooms of his old life, his eyes falling on the ghosts of removed furniture, remembered arguments, burnt toast, bedtime stories. All was quiet and still, yet he could barely hear his thoughts. He heard the front door open behind him. Ann was there but had not seen him yet. He watched her put her bag down on the bare floor, looking at the graceful parallel bending knees just below her red skirt. She straightened up, saw him, and brushed her blonde hair behind her ear.

"I saw your car outside," she said. "Where's Roman?"

"I couldn't get him to come."

"How hard did you try?"

"He's eighteen, Ann. I can't make him do anything."

"I can't believe he didn't go to graduation."

"Have you tried to call him?" Baron asked.

Ann looked away. "He won't speak to me."

"He will," Baron said, "in time."

"I really hate that tone of voice."

"I was only–"

"I hate that 'I told you so' tone. Just because he decided to live with you and not me. You think you're winning or something."

"I don't think anyone is winning here."

"There you go again."

"I can't speak? I can't say anything?"

Ann crossed her arms. The room went hollow and cold. Baron tried to relax. He still hated that she was upset and missed Roman. He looked out the window at a perfect August day.

"He's punishing me for taking the job."

"You think that's the only reason?"

Ann was silent.

"You moved out, Ann. Neither of us knows what's going on with you."

"Nothing is going on with me."

"Nothing. What about the guy at work?"

"What are you talking about?"

"I know, Ann. I know."

"That was nothing."

"If it was nothing, then why are we selling the house? Why are Roman and I living in Coxville? If it's over, then why don't you come home?"

"I can't."

"Why not?"

"Because it's just not home anymore."

There was a knock at the front door, and voices.

"Look. Just come with me and we'll go see Roman together. We'll forget all this ever happened and move on. Go back to the way things were."

"You won't, though," she said sharply.

"Won't what?"

"You won't forget. It's just one of those things that makes you who you are."

"I will. I promise. I just want us to be together again. To be a family."

Ann seemed to break from herself for a moment but regained herself and she backed away. "That would be nice, wouldn't it?"

Baron held his hands out toward her. She looked at them but did not move.

"I just can't," she said.

"Can't or won't?"

"Both."

Baron crossed his arms. "Just give me what I need to sign," he said angrily.

Ann handed a stack of documents to him. He signed quickly and handed them back and, in this exchange, he felt sick in a way he had never known. He stood there and looked at his shoes. He heard Ann exchange pleasantries with the people in the foyer, as if nothing at all had just happened.

The thought of Nora sent a surge of excitement up Roman's spine and made his heart race. The wind blew through his Jeep. The morning sun was drying the puddles left by the early morning rain. He felt a confidence and a keen satisfaction with everything around him. He was finally moving on, something he had told himself to do over and over again. He just had to find the right person. Nora, he was sure, understood. His feeling of elation gave way for a moment, and he noticed a bit of grogginess. He remembered how difficult it had been getting to sleep when he got home, a fantastic new future bouncing around in his mind. And when he finally did fall into a deep sleep, he had had the most fantastic dreams and woken up late. It had been a while since his dreams had been so vivid or so positive. He thought to write them down when he first got up, but by the time he had stumbled around the house looking for something to write on, the dreams had faded.

Roman reached the Coxville city limits, the radio playing loudly, then came around the curve and saw a car parked in his driveway. His stomach lurched. It was Cassandra's car. She was standing on the front porch. Roman saw the whole gross truth of himself. What he saw he didn't like. He was a fiction, a liar, a fake. He turned the radio down and parked his Jeep next to her car in the driveway. Cassandra was wearing an unrecognizable expression. They exchanged a weary glance. He got out of the Jeep and went up to her. He could now see how upset she was, obviously doing her best to hold back tears. A slight quiver was in her voice.

"Hey," she barely got out.

"Hey," he said, moving slowly closer to her.

They hugged each other quickly. The past came rushing back into his mind—his own voice saying so many things, promising so much.

"What are you doing here? I mean…."

"I just came up to see you. How have you been?"

"Right now, not so good."

They stood staring at each other. He felt deceitful and realized how thoughtless he had been.

"Why don't I show you around?" Roman offered.

"It's good to see you" she said.

"You, too," he uttered.

"Sure." Cassandra said quietly.

They went into the house. Cassandra noticed that it looked neglected; the rooms bare, the wood floors dusty. Boxes were everywhere, stacked, ready to fall at any moment. She felt bad for him, and a little of the anger she felt subsided.

"This is it," Roman said looking around, "it's not much." Stalling, he took her through all the small, smelly, dank rooms

"Why did you father move you to this place? It seems so strange."

"I'm trying to figure it out," he said. "Let's go outside."

Roman sat on the steps. Cassandra walked past him and stood at the bottom of the steps, leaning on the railing, her keys still in her hands, clinking, as if at any moment she would leave.

They sat in silence for a while. Cassandra was trying not to look at him directly. Roman was rubbing his face and running his hands through his hair, trying to think of things to say. He covered his mouth with his hands and tried to look her in the eyes. The low hum of the air-conditioning unit was the only noticeable sound.

"You're acting really weird. Maybe I should go," she said, finally.

"No!"

"Why haven't you called?" she asked bluntly.

Roman searched for an answer. He wanted to be honest.

"I …ah… have been kind of caught up here."

"I'm glad to see you're adjusting, meeting some new people."

"Yeah. I've really met a lot of new people. It's been strange at times but…." Roman had to hold back.

"But what?"

Roman shook his head.

"You couldn't find five minutes to call me?"

Roman said nothing, because no words came.

"What about us? I mean, a couple of months ago everything was fine. You said you were going to come back to Seaside every weekend. We were getting along, having fun. Then the next month, you came home just twice. We talk on the phone, and you seem distant. No one ever answers your phone. I figured you just needed time to yourself to get adjusted, so I tried to be cool about it. I feel like some psycho for having to come up here."

Roman stood up and he wanted to say he was sorry and hug her, but he stopped. "No… not at all. You're right," he said. "I really don't know what's wrong with me. I think it shows that you care a lot about us to come up here. It's just, things have been so crazy here. I've been kinda carried away by this new environment. I just haven't had my head on right, I guess. It's been a real diversion from all those bad memories in Seaside."

"How's your dad?"

"He's doing great. He's working in the shop over there," he pointed at the garage on the corner. "Cassandra, I just really don't know what's going on."

"So, what does that mean?" she asked sharply, stiffening and standing up straighter. Roman couldn't recall them having ever argued with each other before.

"I just don't know," he said.

"If you wanted to break up, why didn't you just do it?"

"I didn't want to."

"So, you just thought you would be an asshole until I stopped liking you? Is that it? You don't have the guts to just break up with me. Maybe it's because you feel bad because you made yourself out to be a certain way and then you think you can just ignore me, and I'll go away."

Her voice was intense and full of anger. "Why haven't you come back, like you said you would? Jesus, I can't even begin to start with all the promises you made me. I mean, I know this whole moving the last two months of school has been hard for you and everything else, but you didn't even try to stop it from happening. You just went along with your dad. You should have done something. Something for *us*. I just don't know how things went from the way they were to this." She put her hand on her forehead and her eyes began to tear up.

"I've really been hurting. I've tried to tell you, but it seemed like you just didn't care. I love you, Roman. Do you love me? I'm not feeling it like I did before. Before, I could tell that you loved me. It's something you can just feel. You don't love me anymore, do you? You convinced me that we were meant to be together, and this is how you treat me."

"Cassandra, I'm sorry."

"Is that all you can say? What? You think I can just forget about the last two months? How can I believe anything you say? I had to drive all the way here just to get you to talk to me."

Roman was silent.

"You're the most selfish person I have ever known. The only thing you think about is yourself. You think you can just mope around feeling sorry for yourself."

That was too much. Roman exploded. "What do you want me to say, Cassandra? Nothing has gone according to plan. Everything I have ever wanted just keeps getting fucked. I didn't want to move here. When I found out, I was devastated. It felt like everything I cared about was being torn away from me. And you're right, I have just kinda let it happen. It hurts too much to know when things aren't going to work out," Roman yelled.

"What are you talking about?"

"Long-distance relationships. They never work out."

"But it's only for a little while. Just the summer, and then you're coming back, right?" Cassandra pleaded.

He knew then why he had let go of her. The chance with Nora was what he wanted. He looked away from Cassandra. He realized he wasn't the person he wanted to be, and he was selfish, and the thing with Nora would never work because it started wrong. He wasn't the good guy, he was the bad guy. He had always prided himself on the fact that he was so giving, so self-sacrificing, so morally superior. Here was the stinging, aching proof that he wasn't so nice after all. She was right, he had been selfish, and her knowing it made him want even more for her to leave. She had seen through him, or he had changed. He didn't know which reality scared him more.

"I'm going to ask you one more time."

"Don't do this, Cassandra. Not right now."

"Just answer the question."

Roman shook his head and felt his eyes water. He was determined not to cry.

"Do you love me?"

He sat there, staring into her eyes, and said nothing, which was the same as saying everything. Cassandra couldn't hold the tears back any longer. She covered her eyes and started walking toward her car. Roman watched every movement she made. Her feet. Her legs. Her entire body. He knew he would regret this moment for the rest of his life. Cassandra got into her car, started it, and backed out of the driveway. He didn't move. He could see the pain in her face, and it scared him that he could hurt someone so much. As she backed out of the driveway, he thought of the things he could do to stop her and make her happy. He could make everything right for her. Something deep inside him told him that it would be a lie, that he would be acting and this scene would just repeat itself, a month, maybe two, down the road.

Roman watch her car move out of sight and sat on the steps, numb. It was all so confusing. What if it didn't work out with Nora? He brushed that thought aside. Nora will make this all go away, he told himself. Nora will make everything better. He hated himself for thinking that way. Wasn't Cassandra right? Did he love her? He had, he knew it, but what about now? If he could be thinking about another girl, wasn't Cassandra better off finding someone else? If his love for her was so fragile that it couldn't survive a simple move, then maybe they weren't meant to be together. There was that thought again that troubled him so much. What was "meant to be together" supposed to mean, anyway? Shit. People were always saying it. Saying it like they meant it, or even knew they had a clue as to what it meant. Fuck. What does anything mean?

Augustus came down the stairs from his room. He had a headache and felt dizzy. He had tossed and turned all night. His legs still felt tired, and he held the railing as he came down. It was 11:25. Augustus looked into the living room and saw his mother. The TV was on and she was on the couch sleeping. He went in and watched her sleep and thought about how much he hated Sunday mornings. He knew his father was at church now, seething over their absence, and he knew when Hart came home, he would be in a bad mood. Augustus decided he had to get out of the house soon—before his father got home.

Augustus thought back to his mother's church-going mutiny three years ago. It was an argument between his father and mother he would never forget. They came pretty close to divorcing. Since then, his mother had changed from the woman he knew to the person she was now. She was always sleeping on the couch. He remembered her as hard-working, a good teacher with a sensitive heart, always helping some student who was neglected. She had always been just as busy, and involved in as many things, as his father. Like Augustus, she could never do enough either, he guessed. Hart sucked all the air out of every room he was in. There wasn't enough air left for others to breath. He had to be in charge and involved in everything.

When Augustus had turned eighteen earlier in the year, things had changed. He was no longer forced to come home at night. Hart's relinquishing of these points of contention had led him to become angrier in other areas. He was constantly upset about Augustus's grades and SAT scores, how many hours he had worked that week, or his baseball performance during the season. Hart worried incessantly about his scholarship. After games it was always what Augustus had done wrong and how it was going to affect his future. Hart would then throw the guilt trip on Augustus about how lucky he was and how much had been done for him.

Augustus hated most his father's pompous attitude and constant judgment of everyone. His father often mentioned people in a positive light and would tell the same story about how good this person was over and over. He did the same for people he knew who drank or went bankrupt. There had always seemed, to Augustus, to be many more of the latter kind of people than the former. He wished he could say Hart was a success only because of the things his grandfather had had, but he knew this was a lie. He hated his father's success. All the land he owned, the business, being mayor, and thinking he knew everything. "If you would just do as I tell you," he would say. That always struck Augustus as the wrong thing to say to anyone. After Augustus quit Legion baseball that summer and they had a huge argument, he had tried to avoid his father ever since. Augustus felt bad for Hart because he had the sense that Hart was realizing that everything he had done had not been totally on his own. This realization, Augustus figured, had something to do with his father's anger throughout life. He thought a deep frustration boiled in Hart's subconscious. Resentment—not unlike his own.

Augustus went back into the kitchen. He wondered if he would end up like his mother. He knew he was aimless, and was disgusted with himself. He feared his father was right. He went back upstairs, his head still throbbing. He lay back down on his bed, turned the TV on, and drifted back to sleep.

ELEVEN

The sun-drenched days of the new June summer gave way to a broiling July, and then the burnished orange of August. The long, roasting days flew by in a flourish of parties, days at the beach, and sitting by the pool. The summer excitement came to a quiet end. Roman and Nora were an item now, enjoying the fresh, intimate discoveries that being in the company of one another were bound to reveal.

They were spending every day together; neither had to work so they spent their days finding others who, like them, had nothing else to do. They just did whatever and acted on any and every whim. They biked and walked Nora's neighborhood, had picnics in quaint, neglected parks, went to the mall to window-shop, and visited museums. Mostly they fantasized about the future, the people they would meet, the places they would go. At night they went to movies or rented them and watched them at Nora's house. Their conversations became prolonged, honest, and open. If there were parents out of town and friends were getting together, they made an appearance or were cajoled by friends, other nights, into jumping the fences at apartment complex pools for a late-night swim.

"What was the happiest time in your life?" Nora asked. She and Roman were in the hammock, lying side by side, inside the screened-in porch of her parents' house. A candle was lit, and classical music wafted in through the open French doors. They struggled in the hammock to get comfortable, the screws in the wood creaking.

Roman finally settled, with Nora's head on his shoulder, and thought for a minute about all the happy moments, and a few not-so-happy ones, wandering around in his mind. He figured that the only way to tell the happy ones from the bad ones was to assign them as such, but if they all had led him here, could any of them be truly bad?

"I don't know," he said, his voice soft, lost in reverie.

"Come on, you have to have had a happiest time in your life. You weren't always this uptight, I hope. And you can't say meeting me. That would be too corny."

Roman looked at her when she wasn't aware of it and was surprised how well she already seemed to know him. She asked the strangest questions sometimes and would laugh uncontrollably as he squirmed to answer clumsily. Curiously, he felt he could tell her anything and that was, after all, what he wanted most in a girl. To be able to talk about anything that came to mind, his darkest thoughts or his deepest fantasies.

"Well, I guess it would have to be when I was young and my father and mother and I would go up to the mountains during the summer. I always loved the mountains. It's just so different from the coast. I remember feeling that the air was, I guess, crisper or fresher. I remember taking my shoes off and playing in little mountain streams. My parents both loved the mountains. They didn't have a lot in common, but I always had the feeling that they were really happy when we were in the mountains. They seemed to like each other a lot more there."

"That's pretty cool. I like the mountains, too."

"What about you?"

"My happiest memories are of being on my father's boat. He had this big boat that he restored, and we would take trips on it to little coastal towns. I always loved anchoring the boat and then paddling ashore. There's just something so cool about sailboats. You can go wherever you want; you can explore small, deserted islands. And when you go to a city on the water there are always other boats to look at and the restaurants to go to. We would take bicycles ashore and ride around those old towns, smelling the ocean and fish in the air."

A horn blew on the road out in front of the house. They both looked but could not see who it was. It was late in the day; the sun was setting, an orange-red barely over the treetops. Roman turned his head slightly to see where the sun was and figured there were just a few minutes left in the day.

"What do you want to do tonight?" Nora asked, pushing her hair back behind her ear. She was lying beside him. She nuzzled her head into his neck, closed her eyes, and just listened for him to speak. Roman took a deep breath. Her head moved up with his inhalation.

"Well, it's Friday, there's got to be something going on. We should go out. I heard they were having one last party at the old house down on the river…"

Nora looked irritated. She didn't like the parties at the old house.

"Hey," he said, nudging her elbow.

She gave Roman a funny look. "I'm not going out to that stupid house."

"Why not?"

"I'm just not. Okay?"

"I don't see what the big deal is. Everybody's going to be out there. Don't you want to see everybody one last time before everyone goes off to school?"

"I'd like to see everybody, but I'm not going out there," she said, as if she were thinking of something better to do.

"What? Is it too redneck for you? Are you too sophisticated to go out to an old house and party?" Roman asked.

Nora was distant for a second. Roman could see that he had gotten to her but wasn't sure exactly what about. He was relieved when she gave up and smiled. Nora had a million reasons why she didn't want to go there, but she kept silent. She sat up. "You really think I think I'm too good to go to that party?" she asked.

"Of course I don't."

"Then why did you imply that I am?"

Roman was silent for a minute. She was right. "I was just joking."

"You mean you were picking on me," she said.

"Hey, even I've been called stuck-up," Roman admitted.

"So, you're saying I'm stuck-up."

"Nora… uh… that's not what I mean."

Nora rolled her eyes. "Damn it. I really hate you, sometimes," and pushed him off teasingly.

They kissed and she moved her head back to his shoulder. She should probably tell him the truth, she thought, but she didn't want to ruin the night. She kept quiet, thinking.

Nora looked away. Roman knew something was bothering her.

"What's wrong?" he asked.

"Nothing," she said, shaking her hair back, looking at him with a grin, and rubbing her arms.

"You've got goosebumps," Roman said, brushing her closest arm with his hand. "Are you cold?"

"No," she said, "I was just thinking about something."

"Something good? Something about me?" he asked.

"It's weird. I was thinking about something bad, at first, but then thought about something good and it wiped it all away."

"Well, what were you thinking about?" he asked, his curiosity stirred.

"I don't remember now," she countered quickly.

"The good, or the bad?" Roman insisted.

Nora sat up. "Do you really want to know?" she said emphatically.

Roman braced himself. He put his hands together behind his head. "Yeah."

Nora groaned and withdrew. "I don't want to tell you."

"Why?" Roman ask helplessly.

"Because I want you to be worried about it first," she said.

"You are something else. I guarantee, if you're thinking about it, then I am, too."

"Then who goes first?"

"You do," Roman said. "Because you brought it up first."

"Actually, you did," she said. Roman looked back at her.

"I'm worried about the future," she said, as plainly as she could.

"What do you mean?"

She mocked him. "What do you mean? I thought you said you were thinking about it, too?"

"Oh, yeah." Roman laughed, feeling as if he had slipped one by her. Nora could tell. She ignored it.

"We haven't really talked about it."

"About what?"

This made her angry. Roman could see it, but something small in him was happy about it. He had never seen her upset, nor had she ever been mad at him.

"Would you be serious? Just one second. That's all I ask," she demanded.

"Okay! Okay!" he quickly reassured her. "I'll try."

"College is coming up. You said so yourself. I mean, are we going to see each other?" she paused. "Or are we going to break up?"

"Break up?" he repeated.

"Yeah, break up," she said sternly.

"I didn't know... you were like... you know... my girlfriend," Roman said, teasing.

She hit him on the arm.

"Officially, is what I mean."

"Not your girlfriend?" she asked incredulously. "We've only spent every day for a month together."

"You have a point there," Roman said, tapping his chin with his finger, as if he were adding things up scientifically in his head. Slashing zeroes to nines and carrying ones. "You make a strong case."

Nora started to get up off the hammock. Roman grabbed her around the waist.

"Wait. Nora, wait. I'm just kidding," he said, laughing.

Nora stopped. He loved her so much. Just loved to look at her. He felt so lucky.

"You're just like every other guy. Trying to play stupid. You make yourself out to be something you're not."

"I'm sorry," Roman said, and pulled her close to him.

"I'm going off to State in a couple weeks." She was stern now. "Have you figured out what you're going to do? It would be better if we just end this thing now before someone gets hurt."

"If things ended now I would be hurt," he said quickly.

She seemed to immediately fall back into him. He had regained her trust with swift honesty. Nora was listening now and Roman felt he could tell her what he had wanted to tell her since he first met her. There were so many things he wanted to say, yet he knew it was best to wait. With Cassandra he had said too much too quickly and had hurt her. He was determined not to do that again. He wouldn't be pushy, either, as he had been in the past. Everything would be perfect this time. Strangely, he felt he had the necessary experiences, the relationship tools, to make this one last.

"How about if I went to State, too?" he asked.

"I thought you said you were planning to go back to Seaside?"

"That's before I had a reason to go to State."

"I didn't know you got in. You failed to mention that you applied."

"Do you want me to go to State?" Roman asked.

"Do you want to go to State?" Nora asked.

"Sure," Roman said. "One college is just as good as another."

"So. You're saying you're going to State."

He nodded.

She hugged him. "That's awesome! We're going to have a great time." They held each other and were quiet. "You're sure that's where you want to go to school? You're not just doing it for me?"

"I did apply there."

"I'm serious," she said, squeezing his hand.

"I am, too. I've been thinking about going there for a long time. It's merely coincidence that you're going there as well. My mother wanted me to go there."

"Lucky me," she said, smiling, and watching the ceiling fan turn.

"Yeah. Lucky you," Roman joked.

"Lucky me? Lucky you!" she insisted, sticking her finger into his side where she knew he was ticklish. Roman squirmed.

"Stop! Stop!" he cried. "Stop it! I mean it!"

"What are you going to do?" Nora said in her deep mocking voice.

"I'm gonna smack ya."

"Typical southern reaction. Men smacking their girlfriends," she said, stopping her finger assault.

"You're not my girlfriend," Roman quipped.

"Why? Because we haven't done it yet?"

"No, because I haven't asked you to be yet," he said, twirling her hair with his finger.

"Oh, whatever," she said turning away from him onto her other side, facing away from him.

"Nora. Hey."

Nora said nothing, pretending to be mad at him. She turned back around and Roman put his fingers through her thick blonde hair, moved his lips close to her ear, and whispered, "Nora. Will you?"

Nora started to laugh hysterically. She turned toward him smiling and kissed him. "You're so cute."

"Well?"

"Of course I'll have you," she whispered anxiously in his ear.

"Then it's settled," Roman said with finality.

"Fine by me," Nora responded.

"Can we do it now?" Roman asked.

"Maybe later," she uttered as they held each other tightly. The day was bright and blue around them and Roman could not remember ever being this happy.

Augustus heard his father's footsteps on the stairs. He rose from his bed, turned off the TV, and put a shirt on. Hart appeared in the doorway, the familiar look of disgust on his face.

"Where are you going?" his father asked.

"Out," Augustus said.

"Out where?"

"A friend's house."

"You're not going anywhere," Hart said sternly.

"Who's going to stop me?

Augustus walked toward the door, but his father didn't move. Augustus stopped short of the door. He was several inches taller than his dad, but he had seen his father blow up before, and it had taken five men to hold him back when a player had intentionally taken a cheap shot at Augustus during a Babe Ruth Allstar game. Augustus stopped and shook his head, ready to listen until he couldn't take it anymore. Hart sensed this moment of reluctance in Augustus and tried to resume a normal tone.

"Augustus, look. I just want you to be responsible. You're not showing up for work. Your car looks terrible. You're worrying us sick not coming home. I mean, after all we've done for you, how can you just act like you don't care? You have summer practice coming up soon. You quit Legion. You're doing nothing except being a bum."

"It's always about Legion baseball or football, isn't it? Baseball. Maybe I don't want to play baseball or football anymore."

"What are you talking about? Do you know how many people would kill to play college football? To get a free ride through college?"

"That's just it. What does a scholarship matter, anyway? You can afford to send me to school."

"What's that supposed to mean?"

"It means all you care about is yourself. You just like being up there in the stands with the other dads and all the other crap that you do. You think you own everything and everybody. You think just because you buy me a nice car, I'm supposed to bow down like you're some god. Nothing is ever good enough. I hate working for you at the car lot and when I mention getting another job you talk about firing me.

So I'm just stuck. Damned if I do, damned if I don't. So, you're right, I just don't care anymore."

"I don't know what the hell is wrong with you, but you're going to do something today before you go anywhere. I know what you've been doing. Drinking and doing drugs every night with those lousy friends of yours."

"They're not lousy. You don't even know them. You don't know what I do. What do you want me to do? Cut your grass? Wash your car before I can leave the house? Fuck that! I'm eighteen, I don't have to be your fucking slave anymore."

The slap went across Augustus's face—hard, a ferocious blow. Stunned, Augustus backed away. He rubbed the left side of his face. It hadn't hurt so much as knowing he'd done something so wrong. He regretted immediately cursing at his father. He looked his father in the eye. He had never seen him so angry.

"Don't you ever swear at me," Hart thundered, pointing his finger in Augustus's face.

Augustus turned and ran down the stairs. Sarah was standing up in front of the sofa. She had been listening to the argument.

"Augustus," she called to him as he went by. The door slammed behind him. She watched him hurry out to his car. Sarah listened, horrified, as the tires peeled away on the street.

Hart came down the steps. Sarah eyed him, her hands on her hips, angry. Her words came out in a scream.

"I've had enough of this. Everybody around here is miserable and you just make things worse! He's liable to do anything now. You've upset him."

"What?" Hart yelled back, "I don't care if he's upset."

"There's no telling what he'll do. I don't understand why you just can't relax. You're on his case all day, every day. I can see why he doesn't want to be around you. All you do is criticize. I know. You've been doing it to me for twenty years," she said angrily.

"He's got to learn to be responsible."

"He knows how to be responsible and he's a good kid. He has a lot of friends. He's good to them. He's going through a rough time right now, can't you tell? Ever since he and Nora broke up this last time. Instead of listening you're just pounding away at the same old shit."

"Don't cuss around me, Sarah."

"You can't tell me what words I can use. That's what I'm talking about. You're so damn sanctimonious. You think you're so damn perfect, but everything you have is 'cause of your daddy. What's really bothering you, Hart? You've gotten worse. You're crueler than ever. Why don't you just go talk to him?"

Hart had the painful look of a man bleeding inside.

"Go back to sleep! That's all you ever do, anyway," Hart yelled, and walked out the door.

Sarah finally knew she had to do something. She put on her shoes, went out, and walked down the drive toward the street. She had been silent for too long. She had let Hart's rampages go on for too long. She couldn't let Augustus be treated that way; Hart was driving him away.

Hart and his younger brother had grown up in the shadow of their father. So much so that Hart's brother had left 20 years ago. Augustus Senior had, without trying to, made them hate each other. She remembered those days so clearly, so painfully. Augustus Senior was always trying to make both the boys happy. He always told each of them what they wanted to hear and never the truth. Now, Hart didn't want to hear the truth, he only wanted to hear that he was right. She had tried so many times to get Hart to talk to his brother. Hart wouldn't hear of it. To Hart, Augustus Senior was God himself, and his brother had betrayed them, abandoned them. She tried to think of how long it had been since they had spoken. It's time they stopped acting like children, she thought. She stopped at the street and looked over beyond the dealership to where the old red-tiled garage was. One of the bay doors was open.

She walked through the grass at the bottom of the hill atop which the church sat. She crossed the intersection and wiped a bead of sweat from her brow as she crossed the road. She was on the pavement of Augustus Senior's old gas station. She heard music and a fan blowing. She heard a tool clank against the floor and saw Baron come from behind a raised hood.

"Hey, Sarah!" Baron said, surprised, as his eyes lit up.

"Hello, Baron," she managed, barely holding back tears, her arms crossed, leaning on one leg.

"Wow. You're just as beautiful as the last time I saw you. You haven't changed at all," Baron said, wiping his hands.

"Neither have you," she uttered. "Are you going to hug me or not?" she asked, her arms outstretched.

"I'm all greasy."

"I don't care," she said. "Come here." They hugged. "You have to go talk to your brother," she begged.

"Why? What's wrong?"

"What isn't wrong, Baron? With your father dying, the boys, the two of you across the street from each other, not speaking. You tell me," she demanded.

"We've got a lot of pride," Baron said.

"Yes. You both do. So, what's it going to be?"

"I don't know." Baron shrugged.

"Would you do it for me?"

"I'll do it for you, Sarah."

"He's inside," she said, hugged him one more time, and left him there on the corner.

Baron looked at the dealership he hadn't stepped into in 20 years and a life, unlived, was felt within him, but it passed—yet he still hesitated.

Hart was in his office. He sat down at his desk and flipped through all the paperwork scattered in front of him. There were bills, a title reassignment form, a title, VINs, bills of sale, buyers' guides, receipts, to-do lists, mail, Black Book value lists, invoices, a stack of messages to be returned. Then there was the town's business over on his other desk. He wondered if he was making more enemies than friends as mayor of Coxville. He guessed he would remain mayor until enough of the citizens, the ones who voted, were tired of him. He was already tired of them, but he didn't mind making the big decisions and he didn't mind if everyone didn't agree with him. He picked up some letters of concern. So-and-so was against the new development beside his house, someone else was upset about the crack in the street in front of his home, Bob Klein wanted the Christmas parade held on a certain day. It's August, for Christ's sake, Hart thought. He kept reading. Dawn, one of his tenants, had three kids, was unemployed, and said she couldn't pay her rent until Friday. He looked at the folder he kept of all the people who owed him money, picked it up, and stuffed it in the file drawer where he might not think about it for a few days. He turned on his computer, stared at it for a minute, then powered it off. He pushed away from his desk and leaned back in his chair and thought about how this office had once been his father's. It was different now. His father had only had a small desk back then, piled high with papers. The desk always worried him as he got older because it seemed his father was so disorganized. He wasn't; Augustus Senior would tap the side of his own head and say, "You worry too much, like your mother. It's all in here."

Augustus Senior had always been out in the showroom talking to people shopping for cars or those who just stopped by. The four corners of Coxville's main intersection had changed from when Augustus Senior first started across the street as a boy at his mother's gas station. He had inherited it after his mother died and he had added the garage. He bought the lot on the opposite corner and started a used car business that had eventually become the dealership. Hart remembered as a child the long hours his father worked—sun-up to sundown, usually. Saturdays, too.

On Sunday no one was allowed to do anything. Hart, his brother, Augustus Senior, and his mother went for drives on those Sundays in whatever new car his father had that week. Hart thought often of those happy drives. When he was seven his mother left, and she and Augustus Senior divorced. It was hard for Hart because, at that time, no one's parents were divorced. It was unheard of. Augustus blamed her alcoholism, which led Hart to secretly blame his mother, because he thought his father could do no wrong. Hart had been born when she was eighteen, Baron, less than a year later. Hart imagined it had to have been difficult for an eighteen-year-old with two babies a year apart, but he still couldn't get over her leaving.

Hart looked over at a bill on his desk that said Highland Retirement Home, where his mother lived now, and wondered if that was where he would end up—would he die there?—or would Augustus let him live at home as Augustus Senior had lived with him until he died? Hart stood and walked over to the filing cabinet, opened it, and took out the only family photograph he had of the four of them. He took the large portrait of his father down and slid it behind some boxes in the back room. He rummaged through one of the cabinets in his office and found a smaller framed picture of Augustus Senior, one from his early years in his Navy uniform. He hung it on the wall where the portrait had been, then locked his office door and went out. He looked over at the station and garage on the opposite corner and could see Baron looking back at him. Hart walked out into the lot among the cars and stood. For months he had avoided looking over at the opposite corner. A car stopped at the intersection and turned left up Main Street as another kept straight on out of Coxville. Hart moved closer to the corner and stood there, gazing across the street. Baron walked toward him, past where the gas pumps had been, the ones he had worked at as a boy, and out into the empty drive of the old station. Hart's eyes looked up the hill, toward the church, as he tried to find the courage to utter something. Baron stood, watching for traffic, his hands in his pockets, then crossed the intersection and walked up to Hart. A moment passed and nothing was said. The sun was falling just behind Hart, its color and brightness the orange that can be looked at for only a moment. Baron found words first.

"How are you doing?" he asked.

"Honestly? Not so good," Hart said, and asked, "You want to come over and see the place?"

Baron nodded and they walked up to the dealership.

"The place looks good," Baron said as they approached the main door. Hart held it open for him. There were two large leather chairs that the salesmen sat in against the wall of the offices. Hart sat in one and Baron sat in the other.

"The lot looks to be doing well," Baron said.

Hart only nodded, and Baron nodded too, and both of them looked out the large glass windows of the dealership, just as their father had, and just as the three of them had all those years ago, out at the cars in the lot, and the stop light, always blinking, and the traffic that stopped at it. Both men looked regretful and felt that not a day had passed that they hadn't looked through those very same windows in their memories and nothing had changed, yet everything had changed, and the past was something that dies hard, and maybe they were finally old enough and man enough finally to accept it.

Nora was lying on her bed snuggled under her fluffy white comforter. She was drifting happily off to sleep when the piercing ring of the telephone woke her. She blinked her eyes and looked sleepily at the clock. It was 12:35. Roman had left half an hour ago. Had she been asleep? There were the faint images of dreams in her head but nothing she could recall. The phone rang again. She answered it.

"Hello?"

"Nora."

She knew immediately whose voice it was.

"Augustus, do you know what time it is?" she asked, half angry and the other half feeling something like pity.

"Yeah, I do. I wouldn't bother you if it wasn't important."

Nora noticed there was something wrong in his voice.

"What do you want, Augustus? I thought we agreed not to talk anymore?"

"I know. I know. It's just I can't help…" he drifted off.

"What is it, Augustus?" she asked.

"I need to talk to you. You're the only person I can talk to."

"But it never does any good, Augustus," Nora said.

"Please, Nora, can you meet me outside your house?" he pleaded.

"I don't know, Augustus. My parents are asleep. I don't want to wake them."

"I'm just down the road. Please, Nora," he begged again.

"Have you been drinking?"

"No. I was at Frank's house. I just can't sleep."

"I'll be down in a minute," she huffed, angry at herself.

Nora knew what an awful mistake it was to see him, to talk to him, to relive those old painful feeling, but she still cared about him, and she didn't know why. She was worried about him, she reasoned. Nora wondered about how much a person can still be a part of one's life even after a break-up. How the thought of them lingered and their absence preoccupied every hour, every thought, every decision. She still felt regret and responsible for all that had gone wrong. No. That was not quite it. Maybe she still loved him, but she knew sometimes love didn't matter. Some things just aren't meant to be, she told herself. Some things can't be undone.

Nora snuck down the stairs. She was outside on the porch when she saw Augustus's Corvette pull into the driveway. He quickly killed his headlights. Augustus saw her in the shadows. Nora walked out under the fluorescent streetlight and got in the car. She shivered.

"This better be important," she declared.

"I'm sorry, Nora. I'm just sorry," Augustus said.

"What are you talking about?"

"I'm sorry for everything I've put you through."

She looked over at him, angry, confused, and heartbroken. He didn't have a shirt on, or shoes. There was something wrong in his eyes. He smelled like had been drinking. The window was rolled down and he was smoking. He hadn't looked at her yet. He was just staring ahead. She could see that he now had a beard and his hair had grown long.

She tried to lighten the mood.

"Are you in your bathing suit? What have you been doing today?" she asked, trying to sound as natural as she could. Something in it struck Augustus and he turned to look at her.

"Do you remember the first summer we were together? I ask myself over and over why I didn't go see you up at Governor's School. I just don't understand why I didn't."

"Augustus, that was years ago. You shouldn't worry about that stuff now."

"I know, but don't you wonder how things would have been if I had gone up to see you? I don't know what was wrong with me. I just felt abandoned. I didn't understand why you left. I was so selfish. I felt sorry for myself instead of being supportive. I didn't understand you, Nora."

"Don't worry about it, Augustus. I understand," she said, reaching out and almost touching him on the arm. She stopped herself.

"But when you came back and you were so different, you'd changed so much, and I just felt bad. And then I broke up with you and I don't even know why."

"I really don't want to go over all this again, Augustus," Nora said defensively, recoiling from the memory.

"That's just it. I can't stop going over everything in my head again and again, wondering what I could have done to make things right, to have not hurt you and then having things come back around on me."

"What are you talking about?" Nora asked, confused. She noticed his voice had changed.

"It's started again, Nora. I can't stop thinking. I can't sleep. I feel nauseous. I feel like I should punish myself or something."

"Augustus, you're scaring me," Nora said.

"I'm scared, too. I don't feel like I'm in control and I don't know what to do."

"You should go home and get some sleep," Nora said, anxious now to get out of the car.

Augustus laughed and muttered to himself, "If only, if only."

There was silence. Nora reached for the door.

"I'm sorry, I don't mean to put all this on you like this," he said, reaching out and touching her arm, trying to get her to stop.

Nora looked at his hand on her arm.

"Are you doing okay?" Augustus asked removing it.

"I'm good," she said quickly.

"So, you're dating the new guy now. I see his car up here all the time."

"That's none of your business," Nora said, irritated, and looked away.

"Are you happy?" Augustus asked.

"Don't do this to yourself, Augustus," Nora huffed.

"I just want you to be happy."

"Then you shouldn't have broken up with me all those times," she said quickly and opened the door. She stopped for a moment before she got out and they looked at each other.

Augustus was silent.

"I really have to go," Nora said.

"I'm sorry, Nora," Augustus said again as she got out of the car and closed the door.

Augustus started his car. Nora walked back toward her house, trying not to look back but, just as she was in the shadows of the willow tree by her house, she stopped and watched him leave.

Augustus didn't know how long it would be before he would see her again. They were both going to the same college, but it was a big school. He knew eventually he would see her on some day when she had finally faded from his mind. And on that day when he saw her everything would come back to him, everything he had felt, all the joy and all the pain. He knew for the rest of his life the thought of her would bring on a barrage of memories and "what ifs."

As Augustus drove away, he felt the hollow reality that there was nothing that could be said to make things right. There was nothing that could be done. He felt like throwing up. The darkness in his head was still there. Things happen for a reason, he had been taught, or told, but there was no reason for the way he felt, except that he was supposed to suffer for some reason. That didn't make a lot of sense, either. Had he just wanted things to be too perfect? She didn't trust him anymore and he could sense it and that hurt the most. He had always believed himself a person who could be trusted in love. He had failed.

During Nora and Augustus's talk in her driveway they had not seen the black Mustang drive slowly past them. Roman had left Nora's house and gone to Ronnie's and Dean's to see if anyone was hanging out. Nobody had been there, so he decided to take the long way home and drive back past Nora's house, to look at it and to think about her. Roman saw Augustus's white Corvette in the driveway and an anger swelled up inside him. Augustus was Nora's ex-boyfriend. He had to be. The one she wouldn't talk about. He wondered why he had never seen them in the same place at the same time. Were they getting back together? Relationships took years to get fully over. He had felt it himself. No, Nora cared about him, didn't she? Then the most horrible thought came to him. Were they up in her room? In her bed? Roman almost stopped at her house but he just didn't know what he would say or do. It was all over. He had this feeling before when things were about to be over with a girl. He would call her tomorrow and she would be reticent and changed.

He hit the gas and headed straight for home in a dazed, numb confusion. There was nothing he could do. He felt his eyes grow heavy as he drove home and decided just to get to sleep and hope that tomorrow he would find out that nothing had changed, everything was fine. That she still loved him, and he still loved her. Roman went in his house stumbling like a drunk. He got in bed and hoped that sleep would soon overtake him. He tossed and turned in his bed, somewhere between delirious horrible thoughts and the deep black worry behind his eyelids. Roman didn't dare open his eyes, and somehow fell asleep.

TWELVE

Nora came slowly down the wooden stairs, holding onto the railing and yawning. She had not slept well. Amorphous nightmares had filled her sleep throughout the night. She listened for the sounds of her mother and father as she did every morning. Most mornings, when she reached the first floor, she could hear them talking quietly at the kitchen table, her father with the newspaper and her mother staring out the window, a cup of coffee steaming in front of her.

Nora heard nothing and remembered that it was a Sunday, which meant her father was away working on his boat at the marina and her mother must be outside smoking a cigarette with her morning coffee. Nora looked at the clock and tried to recall the last time she had gotten up so early on a Sunday. She certainly hadn't that summer. In the kitchen there was no sign of breakfast nor, on the porch, was there any sign of her mother. She walked into the living room, then slid the door open to the porch. There was the extinguished butt of a cigarette and an abandoned, half-empty cup of coffee. Her mother had to be near. Nora sat in one of the white wicker chairs and waited. She began to feel the sun's rays, low on the horizon, directly in her eyes. She looked down to the glimmering green lawn, closed her eyes, and felt the warming of the day. She smelled the air, pulled her legs up close to her in the chair, her arms around them, looked at her bare feet, and listened to the birds. She covered her mouth and yawned again. She faintly heard the door open in the kitchen and footsteps moving across the hardwood floors.

Her mother's head popped out the sliding door and startled her.

"Good morning," her mother said, her voice jaunty, her eyes alert, still in her robe. "Something came in the mail for you. I forgot to check it yesterday."

"What is it?" Nora asked. Her mother came out and sat back down in the other white wicker chair. She reached for another cigarette and lit it, still staring at the envelope.

"It's from some foundation," her mother remarked in the middle of a yawn.

"Give it to me. It's the scholarship!" Nora grabbed the envelope and tore it open.

"What does it say?" her mother asked and then sipped her coffee.

Nora read the letter, gave a slight cry of surprise and went over to her mother to show it to her.

"I got it! I got it!" she screamed, jumping up and down.

"That's awesome, sweetie," her mother said, smiling and reaching her arms out to Nora. "You earned it." They hugged furiously for a long moment.

The sudden good news made all the troubling things she wanted to talk to her mother about, especially Augustus's late-night visit, vanish into the luminous possibilities of a still-incomprehensible future.

"So, has it hit you that college is coming up?" her mother asked.

"Not really, I guess," Nora said, but simultaneously remembered and paused, thinking back to her conversation with Roman the previous night.

"I talked to Roman about it the other day," Nora revealed, unable to hide her satisfaction.

"Where is he going to school?" her mother asked.

"Well, he told me he might go to State."

Her mother nodded, taking a drag from her cigarette.

"He seems nice enough," she said, "and level," she added with a smirk.

Nora gave her an annoyed look but said nothing. She knew her mother blamed Augustus for so many things, but Nora wasn't sure that they were entirely his fault anymore. She read the letter again, still beaming. She bent over and kissed her mother on the forehead.

"I'm going back to bed," Nora announced.

Nora went back up to her room and looked through the papers from State on her desk. She laid the new letter on top, thought about the papers for a second, then scooped them all up and carried them to her bed. Among the papers was her dorm assignment with her eventual roommate's name on it—a girl with a normal enough name from out of state—and the course catalog. She examined each paper once more, looking at her class schedule and the pictures of the campus on the cover of one of the pamphlets.

Nora wondered what her roommate would be like. She read the name again and tried to imagine what she might look like. As Nora lay there, she thought of how this house had been so much a part of her life. In a couple of weeks, she would be moving out and into a gigantic dorm on campus. Nora felt anxious. It was going to be such a shock, so many new people. She knew she would be back on weekends and holidays, but already she was missing her home, the last four years, a whole era of her life over. Nora's thoughts drifted, shifting from quiet moments, movies watched on the couch, her teachers, her classes, football games, proms, pep rallies, homecoming parades, parties she had been to, in The Pines and Brook Valley, and all the friends she would miss. Nora's house had always been a hub of activity. Everyone liked hanging out there. Her parents were pretty cool, as far as parents went, without being annoying. Frank, always trying so hard to impress her mother, Tripp always looking through her mail, Betty sitting with her leg hiked over the arm of the living room chair—her favorite position. The cool days when Nora would open all the windows and play her mother's old records and wonder if she was so different from other girls her age, and what her mother was like at her age, and where her biological mother was. Nora wondered if that woman ever thought about her. As she listened to her mother's music, she wondered why it sounded so much like the past looked to her. It would just be her parent's house soon, not hers anymore, and she wondered how much they would miss her.

Nora thought again of her biological mother and father. Would they be proud and excited about her going to college? Nora wondered if her real parents had been to college and, if so, where had they gone. Had she exceeded their abstract expectations? Did they have any expectations for the child that they had given up, or had she been forgotten—repressed into a non-memory? Did they think or worry about her? Whatever could have been the reason for their abandonment of her? Nora began to feel sad. She pushed those thoughts away with thoughts of college and, before she could dwell on it, she was asleep again.

Nora woke and looked at the clock. Her first thought was of Roman. She got out of bed, went over to the phone, and dialed his number. It rang until the machine beeped.

Roman was on the sofa in the living room flipping aimlessly through the channels. He had been lethargic all morning. After seeing Augustus's car at Nora's last night, he was in an anxious state and couldn't be still. Surely Nora would call and tell him everything was fine. He waited for the phone to ring. Roman stood up suddenly, deciding he couldn't just feel sorry for himself, he had to do something, he had to get away, get his mind off it. Roman grabbed the keys to the Mustang and went over to the garage. He figured Tripp was home. As the door shut behind him, he missed the ring of the phone.

Nora tried to call Roman throughout the afternoon. She went out with her mother, shopping for clothes and school things. The city roads were calm with the restless, sweaty pleasure of a humid August day. The mall was a vast, cool oasis of cheerful faces and footsteps, people happy to be out of the heat. They ate first at a table in the wide food court, then went from store to store, commenting back and forth about this dress or blouse. They always enjoyed each other's company.

When Nora arrived home, she took her new clothes up to her room to try them on again and put them away. She turned the TV on and crawled on her bed to look through her school stuff once more. She started watching an afternoon movie and drifted off into sleep, feeling a delirious ease that came only with the alleviation of some prolonged misery, as if something which had held on to her for too long had itself, suddenly, let go. At 7 p.m. Nora made one last phone call to Roman's house. She wondered, frightened for the first time, if he was there and just not picking up. He must have heard her message by now. Nora dialed Frank's number, but his mother only said that she didn't know where he was. She then dialed Betty's number.

"Hello," Betty answered.

"Have you seen or heard from Tripp or Roman or Frank?" Nora asked abruptly.

"Nora? No. Why, Nora? What's going on?"

"Not much. I'm just getting a little worried because I can't reach Roman," she said with a slight shudder.

"Did you call him? I'm sure he's just outside or with Frank or Tripp somewhere."

"I just have this strange feeling. Is Tripp there?" Nora asked.

"No."

"Do you think he's with Tripp?"

"Tripp, Dean, and Ronnie are all at the beach today. They went to go look at apartments or something."

"Do you know when they're getting back?"

"I don't know. Tripp told me later this evening," Betty said.

"Later this evening?" Nora gasped.

"What's wrong?" Betty asked.

"I don't know. It's nothing," Nora sighed heavily into the phone and sat down.

"About what? Did you guys have a fight or something?" Betty asked.

"Well, Roman and I were hanging out last night and after he left Augustus came by," Nora confessed.

"He didn't," Betty gasped.

"He did."

"What did he want? Why did you let him come over?"

"I don't know. He caught me off guard. He was in the neighborhood. I guess he just wants to torture me some more? But I just feel rotten about it, and I don't know whether I should tell Roman."

"Have you ever told Roman about Augustus?" Betty asked.

"I've told him that I was in a serious relationship for a while and that I got hurt. But Roman never wanted to know any names. He said it didn't matter and he didn't want to know any names so he wouldn't get jealous."

"So, do you think Roman knows anything about you and Augustus? Do they even know each other?" Betty asked

"I've never seen them together. Wasn't Roman sort of like Tripp's new best friend?" Nora asked.

"From what Tripp says, he's barely seen Augustus this summer. I think Tripp's kind of upset because they once were such good friends. Augustus has changed a lot, Nora. He doesn't seem like himself. We don't talk about him around you," Betty said.

"I know. He looked terrible last night."

"I wouldn't worry," Betty said, trying her best to comfort her friend.

"I won't, but do you know where Roman lives?"

"You don't know where he lives?" Betsy asked, astonished.

"He acts kind of strange about where he lives or something because he lives there with just his dad. I've never been there."

"He lives across the intersection from Augustus's dad's dealership in Coxville."

"Augustus's dad's car place?" Nora asked.

"Yeah, isn't that weird?"

"What's weird?"

"You know, how their names are both so strange, and that they live so close."

"Betty, what are you talking about?" Nora demanded. She started to remember that Augustus had told her that he had grown up in a house at that intersection. He had shown her the house one day when they had been at the car dealership.

"It never seemed strange to you that their first names are so unusual and they have the same last name?" Betty asked.

"What?" Nora exclaimed, feeling dizzy, as if she had been whacked in the head by something.

"Nora. You didn't know their last names were both Forlines? Think about it, Roman and Augustus? Augustus's grandfather's name was Augustus. Those aren't your everyday names."

"I know Roman's last name is Forlines, but isn't he from the beach?"

"I just found out where Roman lives last week and you and him have been MIA for a month," Betty said.

"So? Do you think he and Augustus are related, or something?" Nora asked, baffled by the possibility.

"I don't know. Nobody does. Nobody wants to ask," Betty remarked.

"What do you mean nobody? Who else thinks they're related?" Nora demanded.

"Just about everyone's been wondering since he moved here, Nora. Everyone's been waiting to find out, now you're dating Roman."

"What?" she cried. "How could I not know about this?"

"I guess ever since school let out and people have barely seen each other. Maybe gossip is moving a little slower than usual?"

Nora felt nauseous and thunderstruck. Had she cut herself off so much from the world, trying to avoid Augustus, that she hadn't even picked up on something so important? "Just about everyone."

How, she wondered, could everyone else know this and she hadn't realized it?

"I'm going to go by there and find out what is going on," Nora announced.

"Will you call me when you find out?" Betty asked.

Nora hung up the phone. She stood frozen for a minute and stared at her family portrait hanging on the wall, then she grabbed her keys and hurried out the door. She had to find Roman and figure out what was going on. She drove hurriedly to Coxville, remembering all those times she had gone there to see Augustus. The town had become so familiar to her. Maybe that was it. The puzzle of the summer was starting to fit together, and it worried her. There had always been something familiar about Roman that she could not understand. Roman. She said his name in her head. She hoped that everything was just a misunderstanding. They happened to have the same last name, was all. As she passed the sign for Coxville she worried she would see Augustus. The town was so small. Nora remembered seeing him so many times, passing him driving, feeling ignored and rejected and crying afterward. Augustus. What was wrong with him, she wondered—what's wrong with us?

She saw the car dealership and looked across the street, where she saw Roman's Jeep sitting in front of the small house Augustus said he had grown up in. She pulled into the driveway, got out, and went up to the door. She knocked. The door opened and Nora felt relief. But it wasn't Roman. It was an older man, wearing jeans and a T-shirt, silver temples and brown hair. A future version of Roman, she thought. The same kind eyes, face, and undisturbed expression, mysterious in a way, that Roman always had, the lips thoughtful and held tightly together. He opened the door.

"Hello, young lady. Can I help you?" he said.

"Hey, I'm Nora," she said, and held out her hand. He shook it lightly.

"Hey, Nora," he said. "I've heard so much about you. I'm Baron Forlines."

"You just said 'Forlines,' didn't you?" she asked.

"Yes."

"Oh, God. Mr. Forlines, I'm looking for Roman."

"I'm sorry; I don't know where he is. I just got home."

"You don't have any idea where he might be?" she asked.

"Not a clue. His Jeep is here, so he must be out in the Mustang. Maybe over at what's-his-name's house."

"Tripp's? No, Tripp is out of town," she corrected him quickly.

"Hmm. I guess he's probably riding around."

Nora looked out at the road, wondering what to say next. "I know this might seem like an odd question, Mr. Forlines, but are you related to the Mr. Forlines across the street?"

"He's my brother," Baron said.

"He's your brother?" Nora asked.

"Why do you ask?"

"No reason. Could you, if you see Roman, tell him I'm looking for him?" she said quickly.

"I sure will," he said

Nora turned and started to hurry away.

"Hey," he called to her. She stopped and turned.

"How's he doing?"

"Who?"

"Roman," he said. "I haven't met many of his friends and I really don't see him a lot. Is he doing okay?"

Nora thought the question was really nice.

"He's doing really well, as best I can tell. He's made a lot of new friends. I think he's fine."

"You'll see to it, then?" he said, smiling.

"I'll try," she smiled back, as she got into her car. As she pulled away Baron was still standing on the porch watching her. He waved and she waved back.

"How did you know we were out here? We just got back from the beach," Ronnie said before taking a hit off the joint he held in his fingers. He tried to hand it to Dean, who shook his head no and gulped from his beer. Ronnie mumbled to himself and hit the joint again.

"I was just cruising around," Roman said, taking the joint from Ronnie and handing it over his head to Frank. They were sitting on the steps leading up to the porch of the abandoned house. Roman sat back, his elbow propped up on the next step.

"You don't want any?" Frank asked, exhaling a huge plume of smoke.

"Nah, man. I got too much on my mind," Roman admitted.

"Like what?" Frank asked through a cough.

"Look! Someone's coming," Ronnie announced.

"It sounds like Augustus," Dean noted.

The name made Roman immediately stiffen.

"Oh, shit," Tripp uttered.

"What do you mean by that?" Dean asked.

Ronnie looked at Roman, then at Tripp, who just shrugged. The Corvette came up the drive and stopped beside Roman's Mustang. Augustus got out and took his time looking at the black car.

"Cool car," Augustus said.

"Thanks," Roman managed.

"Hell, yeah, it is," Dean said. "Where the hell did you get that thing, anyway?"

Augustus stopped at the bottom of the steps and looked at the four guys sitting there. He was nervous and could feel his heart racing. Roman thought Augustus did not look like the same guy who had intervened on his behalf on graduation night; he looked tired and weak. He still possessed confidence, but his dark hair was longer, and he had grown a thick black beard. Roman wondered what was going on with him. Was he trying some new hippie thing? Something was wrong, and Roman felt the urge to help, to ask him what was going on, but he remembered seeing Augustus's car at Nora's and said nothing. Roman realized that, except for that Saturday night during Junior/Senior, they had never spoken.

It started to occur to Roman that perhaps nothing had happened the night before. He wanted to talk to Nora as soon as possible. Not calling her today, he now realized, had been the wrong thing to do. He had let his imagination run amok again.

"It's my dad's car," Roman replied.

"He doesn't mind you driving it? It must be worth a lot of money."

"What the hell is that thing, anyway?" Dean asked.

"Yeah, what is that thing?"

"It's a Mustang," Augustus announced.

"It's not like any Mustang I've ever seen," Tripp said.

"My grandfather had an old, rusting one just like it," Augustus said, looking back at it. "It's a 1969 Boss 429."

"429? What's that?" Tripp asked.

"The size of the engine," Roman said.

"Oh yeah, you mean cc's," Tripp agreed.

Roman nodded.

"That's a lot of horsepower," Ronnie remarked.

"That motherfucker just looks mean," Dean said.

"You out cruising around, too?" Frank interrupted, asking Augustus.

Augustus nodded.

Roman and Augustus glanced at each other when they thought the other wasn't looking in the dark of the night. Finally, Roman looked right at Augustus and felt him looking back. Neither moved or breathed for a second.

"Yeah, I couldn't find anybody so I just thought I would stop by, you know. How did you like the campus? Did you find an apartment near the beach?" Augustus asked.

"It was all right, I guess," Ronnie said.

"Just all right?" Augustus asked. "You're going to be living there soon. I hope it was better than that."

"It's fine. I mean, I'll be near the beach," Ronnie said.

"Roman's from down there," Tripp added.

"What about you?" Ronnie asked Augustus. "Shouldn't you already be at State? I thought you were going to try and walk on the football team?"

Augustus shrugged his shoulders and took a swig from his beer. He sat the rest of his six-pack on the ground. He looked up into the night sky, looking for the comet, but couldn't see it.

"If I got hurt, I'd lose my baseball scholarship. So, I figured why risk it? Besides. I'm going to have some fun this semester."

"Yeah, man. I'm so ready to get out of this place," Tripp said.

"Man, you'll be back here in a couple weeks partying with the high school kids again," Augustus said.

"No way, man," Tripp said, shaking his head.

They all laughed and, as the thought drifted away, there was silence again. Only the sound of beers being tipped back and drags on cigarettes. Augustus finished his cigarette and flicked the butt into the grass.

"You and Roman should race. I bet that old Mustang would whoop your ass. That's better than just sitting here yapping," Tripp said suddenly, then immediately regretted it.

"You want us to race now?" Augustus asked.

"I don't know about that," Roman said.

"Dude, don't be a wuss. If I had a car like that, I would be racing everybody. And besides, that's the only car I've seen that looks like it could beat that Corvette," Dean said.

"That car would fall apart," Augustus said, eyeing Roman.

Roman ignored him and lit another cigarette.

"What do you say, Roman?" Dean goaded him, "sounds like a challenge."

Roman shook his head again.

"It would have been a good race, is all I'm saying. How about a short one? We'll just see who gets off the line fastest."

Again, Roman shook his head no. Augustus remained silent.

"It's time for me to get home, anyway," Roman said.

"Yeah, I gotta get home, too," Dean said.

"Are you gonna stay, Augustus?" Tripp asked.

"Nah., I think I'll head over somewhere in Martinsboro," Augustus said.

Dean, Ronnie, and Tripp all headed for Tripp's Accord. Roman reached in his pocket for his keys. He took one last glance over at Augustus and the thought came to him to say something. After the fight he owed him that, he figured, but Augustus was already in his car. Roman opened the door of the Boss and slid into the old leather seats, feeling relieved that he had been able to keep his cool. He was still worried about Nora and what might have happened between her and Augustus. Ronnie, Dean, and Tripp in the Accord pulled out and went down the road, followed by Roman in the Boss, then Augustus in his Corvette.

The dust kicked up on the dirt drive of the old house made an impenetrable yellow fog in front of Roman. He slowed down to keep the dust off his father's car. The red taillights of the Accord disappeared. Roman continued on slowly, looked in his rearview mirror, and saw that Augustus was right on his bumper. Roman regretted not saying something to Augustus. What would he say that wouldn't sound like he was trying to start something? Seeing Augustus's car at Nora's house had made him feel he had been betrayed, somehow. His instincts were impulsive and savage, but he remembered that Augustus had not seemed aggressive, just interested and a little pathetic.

Roman slowed at the edge of the road for the final bump that at the end of the drive. He turned the Mustang left onto the blacktop.

His headlights reached far into the dark distance. There was no sign of the Accord. Roman pressed the gas slowly and turned the dial on the radio with the tip of his finger. Behind him, Augustus's white Corvette had made the same turn and was still on his bumper. Roman pressed his accelerator a little more to put some distance between them. He looked into the mirror to see Augustus, but he couldn't see anything. It's only a couple miles to Coxville, he thought. He must live somewhere around there, Roman figured.

Suddenly, the headlights in his rearview mirror became brighter and Roman heard a tremendous roar from Augustus's Corvette. The Corvette was right on his bumper. The lights swung around him, and the Corvette was now beside him. Roman looked over. Augustus looked over and smiled as he started pulling ahead. Roman, startled, feeling an adrenaline rush, did the same and slammed his accelerator to the floor. The blood thumped through him, overcame him, and reason was lost. The Boss started to get closer to the Corvette, but it wasn't enough. Roman hit the clutch and slammed the four-on-the-floor back into third. The Boss crouched back on its wide rear tires. Roman's head went forward and he felt he had lost any chance when, suddenly, the car reared up and tore forward as though shot from a cannon. His head snapped back into the head rest, and he gripped the wheel with everything he had. The white Corvette was just half a car length ahead. Roman looked down at the speedometer as it climbed. Fifty five. Sixty five. Seventy five. The engine roared, a great, rich baritone. Roman could hear nothing else. The car started to feel loose, and he began to hear small squeaks and rattling. He wondered if he ought to be pushing this old car so hard. Eighty. He was next to Augustus. Roman risked a quick look over to see if Augustus would back down. He wished he would. He turned his eyes forward again. Still they were side by side. Eighty five. Roman looked ahead for the guys who had left before them. He felt they should have caught up with them by now. Then it occurred to him that they, like so many others that summer, had taken the opportunity and sped down this same stretch as fast as they could for thrills. They were long gone. Roman thought for a second about letting up—letting Augustus go around him. Letting him win. He didn't. Ninety eight. The Boss was getting harder to keep on the road; the steering was loose, the car vibrated, and the hood shook. He had to grip the wheel with all his strength just to keep it on the road. The Corvette started to pull ahead and Roman realized that he had been holding off. He tried to press the pedal through the floor. He looked at the needle again and couldn't believe how fast he was going. That was when he saw it. Headlights coming toward them. Roman slammed on his brakes. He saw the white Corvette swerve right into his lane. The oncoming headlights went to his left, flashed by his eyes, and went off the road. He locked up the brakes and the Boss came to a sideways screeching stop. Roman looked into his rearview mirror with horror as he saw red lights tumbling over and over.

THIRTEEN

Hart rose at 5:00 a.m., as he did every day. This morning was dark and quiet. He left Sarah in their bed and went into the kitchen to read the paper, but he couldn't focus on the day's trifling news. He got in his truck and headed out to the farm Augustus Senior had left to Baron. He drove past the wooden fences of the pastures and took the long gravel road up to the big barn. He fed his horses, swept out the shop, turned on the radio, and tried to think of what he might do that morning before church. The sun was peeking just over the horizon, and he stopped and looked at it for a while. He got back into his truck, went down the road, and took a right on Forlines Road, to look once again at where the accident had happened a week before. He slowed down as he came to the curve where he had first seen the car flipped over.

Hart just knew Augustus was going to be dead when he got the call about an accident from the sheriff. He had worried so many nights about getting such a call and wondered how he slept at all. Thank God, he said to himself that night when he saw Augustus alive. But, Nora! He had always liked her and had hoped she and Augustus would settle down and get married one day. He moved on past the curve and took the dirt road down to the old farmhouse, the house he and Baron had grown up in.

After Baron left, Augustus Senior had abandoned the house, rented out the fields, and moved to Coxville to the big white house Hart now lived in next to the dealership. Hart couldn't remember the last time he had been out to the house and wondered how he could have forgotten about it. Time, he decided, time forgets for a while. Hart went up to the house and stood on the porch. He could tell that people had been there. Empty beer cans, trash, and chairs were everywhere. It was a good house. He thought about the days growing up here, better days, when he and Baron were just boys, and their mother was around. They had played in the yard, gone fishing down by the river and, when they were older, plowed fields and put in tobacco with Augustus Senior. And then there was Vietnam; he and Baron had gone off to fight, and when they got back they were both different, but Baron had always been a little more different, never liked playing second fiddle, never liked living in the shadow, and never liked Coxville at all. He was a lot like their mother, Hart figured.

Somehow, Augustus and Roman had found their way to the lost home of a past generation even as their fathers had made so many mistakes, trying to keep them apart. Some unknowable force had drawn them to a past they knew nothing about—or maybe it was all circumstance. And Hart knew, in a way that is hard for anyone to fathom, that he was the most responsible.

Augustus parked behind the church and went around to the front brick steps that led up to the sanctuary. He turned and looked out at the town sprawled beneath him. A car stopped at the town's only stoplight, the sun reflected off the windshields of the new cars of the dealership and the rusty old Phillips 66 sign still swung from a pole in front of the service station. The car turned up Main Street and its disappearance left, as the only movement in Coxville, a gusting wind in the large oaks up the hill behind the church. The intersection was empty now and there was only the permanent stillness of the water tower. Down Main Street, the sidewalks were empty, the store front signs read "Closed," and the town was silent, waking to the hazy orange of August. He glanced once more at the town, felt the despair of the familiar, then turned, climbed the red brick stairs, and went inside. He could hear the organ playing. One of the greeters at the door handed him a program. They nodded at each other and Augustus went in. The church was unusually full for a Sunday morning in Coxville.

Inside, he looked for Roman. Augustus felt every eye turn toward him as he entered. Roman glanced over his shoulder, saw him, and waved him over. Augustus went and sat next to him.

When Augustus and Nora had first started dating his sophomore year, the church had been a large part of his life. She had never gone to church except on special occasions or with girlfriends. Nora enjoyed it. When they were 16 there had been a youth group, most of them in high school who really didn't fit in, and some high school graduates who hadn't gone off to College who still lived at home the same habits and friends. Those were the days before Augustus had started drinking and partying so much with his other group of friends. The "youth group," as they were called, met on Sunday and Wednesday nights to hang out in a way that didn't require drinking. It had been a safe haven of sorts for those few who were not really into partying. They had a great time in those days. They went to the mall as a group and on Christmas they watched *It's a Wonderful Life*. In February there was the ski trip.

When Augustus and Nora broke up the first time, he quit going to church and youth group altogether. He remembered the night Nora had been baptized and joined the church. He remembered best those bright, sunny, early days of his first real experience with love and associated those feelings most with the church he was now in. He remembered how innocent he thought himself to be back then—so naive and rigid in his beliefs. It was amazing to him how much he loved her—and the realization was overwhelming.

The sanctuary seemed filled to its high ceiling with the thoughts of her that now entered his head. The little moments they had shared came to him as tiny pictures, images and times that he wished he could go back to and relive. He had always believed that, in the end, they would be together and get married and have children and live the perfect life. Live to old age, watch their children grow up.

The family pew was different this morning. On the far end was Hart, who was leaning over whispering into Sarah's ear. It was strange because it had been a long time since Augustus had seen the hint of smiles between his mother and father. Next to Sarah was his Uncle Baron. Then there was Roman. They made room for him. The choir rose and began singing; the service had begun.

After the service Baron and Hart stood side by side in front of the church, mingling, smiling, and shaking hands with other church members. An older woman came up to them. "I'm so glad to see you boys together again. I remember when you were just little things playing around that store down there when me and my husband would stop to get gas. You both have gotten so big and handsome. My…that was so long ago. Your father would be so happy to see you two here in church together. I remember how he would beam every Sunday with the two of you lined up beside him."

The graveyard was behind the church, between the parking lot and the wooded area that eased down the slope toward the road. Augustus, leaving Roman, hurried out of the church and walked quickly around the corner. He wanted to avoid the questions of how he was doing. His hands were clenched in his pockets as he walked along the back side of the church. He looked down at the freshly cut grass. Opening the small gate to the graveyard he looked over his shoulder to see if anyone had followed him. He had come to church that day hoping that it would make him feel better. It had not.

The cemetery was silent and still. It wasn't very large, but there were a few ornate headstones. He came first to his grandfather's stone. Though Augustus Senior had been a giant in the town, his stone was small, with only his name, dates, and a short epitaph. Augustus read it: "A Loving Father."

He thought for a minute and walked slowly over to the other grave he had come to visit. He stopped in front of it and sat down, his arms around his knees. There was a dogwood tree over him so that he was comfortable in the shade of the hot afternoon sun. He looked around at the blue sky and the way the colors of the landscape were so bright and vivid. Thinking back, he could not remember the last time he felt so alone, and so awful, and so awed by the magnificence of the world in a way that Nora would have understood. She would never again be able to do what he was doing now. He read the granite stone again and realized it was the name that stood out so much and the dates. They seemed to say this, and only this, is when there was life. It wasn't true. Augustus still felt that she was alive. They say people live on in memories. It was true that people do, but there was more to it than that. There was so much of her in him now that he didn't know where he stopped, and she began. He wondered what it was going to be like thinking of the horrible tragedy every day for the rest of his life. Would he be able to sleep? Augustus wondered how he had ever been able to live without her. He heard footsteps behind him.

"Do you think about her a lot?" Augustus asked the person behind him.

"Seems like every second," Roman said.

"I killed her," Augustus wept.

"You didn't kill her, Augustus. *We* killed her."

Augustus looked at him.

"You don't understand. I just couldn't help myself. I just couldn't accept things. I made her cry so many times. I loved her, and then I would hate her, and I don't know why. I didn't know what to do, and I tried so many times to let go, to let her have a better life, but I just kept coming back to her. I was so weak…always so weak."

He was crying now, and Roman knelt and put his hand on Augustus's shoulder.

"Augustus, everything is going to be fine. None of us know what the hell we're doing. It was an accident. You have to accept that."

"I didn't have to race you that night. I didn't have to try to show off."

"Augustus, you can't 'what if' yourself like that. It'll drive you nuts. I know. I didn't have to speed up beside you. It's not fair for you to think it was only your fault. There's plenty of blame to go around. I mean, what if our parents had told us who we were? Then this all would have been different. Jesus, Augustus! I just don't know."

Roman held back tears of his own.

"I don't understand all of this," Augustus said.

"If only they had told us."

Roman was only barely beginning to understand the vast conspiracy that had brought him and Augustus there to that cemetery. How things could have been different. It was wrenching to think about.

Roman and Augustus remained in the graveyard for a while and said nothing. Roman worried more for Augustus than for himself. It was almost an impossible sense of fear and sadness that he felt inside himself. As he stood there, staring at Augustus sitting on the ground in front of him, he had the overwhelming sense that, while his grief was immense, he knew that Augustus's had to be greater. Knowing this he held back tears in that moment, not for Nora, but for Augustus. He had already cried tears for Nora and knew he would again. Roman's heart went out to Augustus, a guy so much like himself. A bleak fear rose as he remembered this friend who had stood up for him when he didn't even know him, confided in him at the beach, and, when he knew that Roman had been seeing his ex-girlfriend, whom he probably still loved, had been decent.

Roman turned without saying anything and left the graveyard. He left Augustus to his solemn vigil, knowing that it would take them all some time to get over it—each in their own way. He walked along the side of the church until he reached the front. The small gathering had dispersed, and the parking lot was empty except for his old Jeep and Augustus's Corvette. Roman stopped in front of the church, feeling a great blast of heat from the sun, and considered the irony of how beautiful the day was and how indifferent it was to the lives and tragedies of people.

Looking to the right, he realized just how high the hill was and how strangely it stood in an area that was mostly flat. He had seen this church so many times and never realized that this was the church of the family he had never known. Looking out, he realized that it was a wonderful view of the little town that he now knew held a greater significance. Roman had felt his entire life that something was lost. He wasn't angry with his father for keeping things from him, but he still did not understand why things had been the way they were.

At last, he had found a sense of who he was and where he was from. And then, he began to think again of Nora.